WAX, V

& M ɪ

MENOPAUSAL

BITS

CHAPTER ONE

Reader I'm divorcing him

My name is Ann. Not regal Anne, just plain, boring, unexciting Ann. It's been some time since I last updated you on my adventures...I am she of the hair remover cream allergy, the burnt bellend and the catalogue of dating catastrophes as long as your arm. As you know, after kissing a fair few frogs, I finally found my prince in the delectable Dr Gorgeous, Archie, now my husband and Father to our beautiful son Jude. I say 'my husband'. He's actually soon to be my ex-husband and I can't fucking wait.

We'd been married for fifteen years when things started to get strange. Almost overnight he went from the perfect husband and Father to a stranger who just happened to live in the same house. He had been promoted to A&E Consultant so of course he was going to be busier but he was barely ever here. He had started to take a lot more care over his appearance...he was naturally gorgeous and seemed to get more attractive as he got older so he didn't need to try too hard. His skin care routine became better than mine and his wardrobe was filling with clothes a twenty year old would wear...I didn't have the heart to tell him ripped jeans made him look like a twat and I was half expecting him to start wearing a clip on ponytail. It felt like he was trying to reclaim his youth and I did put it down to his age...until the day he bought the sports car. When he surprised us all by pulling into the drive in a red, open topped, vintage Ferrari I knew something wasn't right. Jude was naturally delighted, he was going to look so cool being dropped off at school and his mates would be 'well jell' but I was furious. There was no discussion, Archie didn't ask my opinion he just went out and splashed the cash. He didn't want to discuss it with me, he worked hard and he had rewarded himself...surely I couldn't begrudge him that. I didn't begrudge him anything. It was the way he had just done it like I didn't exist that pissed me off.

A couple of days after the car incident I got my answer. There was a knock on my door and I opened it to find Ryan standing on my doorstep. He had stayed with Miss Fucking Perfection Personified all these years and they had become a constant presence in our lives. After our Mexican bump off at the antenatal class I didn't see the delightful Camilla again until Jude started nursery. Camilla and Ryan had indeed had a little girl...Lola. On Jude's first day, I entered the playground to be greeted by Camilla who literally snarled at me and turned her back. As I predicted when we were pregnant Lola was dressed head to toe in pink and covered in bows and sequins. I tried to avoid Camilla at drop off and pick up time but in a twist that could only have been dreamed up by the universe taking the piss, Lola and Jude became best friends. They progressed through nursery and school together so Ryan and Camilla were always around. Well I say Camilla, it was mainly Ryan. As soon as Lola ditched pink, Camilla lost interest. Miss Fucking Perfection Personified had to maintain her glamorous exterior and was forever jetting off abroad to get the latest cosmetic procedure and now as our children were coming to the end of high school she looked twenty years younger. I had gone from sucking in my stomach when I saw an attractive man to sucking in my stomach whenever I saw Camilla. I hadn't aged too badly and with the onset of my menopause I had finally developed a cracking pair of tits. I had some lines on my face...but every line had a tale to tell and my greying hair could be easily covered with hair dye. I was embracing middle age and looked to the future with confidence until that fateful day.

As soon as I opened the door to Ryan I knew something was wrong. He looked pale and emotional. He hadn't even stepped inside the house before he dropped the bombshell that was going to turn my life upside down;
'They're having and affair Ann. Archie and Camilla, they've been at it for months.'

In that one sentence my world fell apart...but in my heart I knew it would happened. That fucking awful woman had haunted me for years. Ryan was distraught...fuck knows why? Camilla had brought him nothing but misery. He showed me a swathe of messages that they had sent each other and it was undeniable...they were at it like fucking rabbits. It was no wonder Archie was always too tired for sex, Camilla had been riding him like a thoroughbred. The messages made me sick to the pit of my stomach and as I read them out aloud, Ryan began to cry;

'She's never been good enough for you, Archie...but never mind you've upgraded now.'

'Doctor, Doctor I have a fire between my legs that only you can extinguish.'

'You really are the biggest boy, Archie. Be quick my love tunnel is waiting.'

Fucking 'love tunnel'? What on earth had happened to my strong and faithful husband? I'd seen enough. I told Ryan to pull himself together as we were going to plan a co-ordinated response...even after all the shit that woman doled out on a daily basis Ryan was absolutely devoted to her. Archie had told me he was away overnight on a course and Camilla had told Ryan she was having a girly meet up with some old friends at a hotel out of town. I think we could safely assume that meant they were together. A plan quickly began to formulate. Ryan would call Camilla and tell her he wanted to send a surprise gift for her and her friends to enjoy. Camilla would definitely give him the name of the hotel she was in...she loved receiving gifts and would never in a million years consider Ryan was on to her.

As predicted Camilla fell for Ryan's story and we sat in silence as we drove to the beautiful five star hotel that my husband was clearly paying for. I think it was one of the longest drives of my life and I ran through every scenario in my head. I swayed from telling him to fuck right off and never darken my doorstep again to trying to forgive him and make our marriage work. We had been together for so long and surely everyone is entitled to make one mistake but when that mistake is not only shagging Miss Fucking Perfection but allowing her to refer to you as 'Archiwoowoo' there's no coming back from that...ever! By the time we arrived at the hotel Ryan had started to get angry...really angry;

'I'm sorry Ann, I know he's your husband but I'm going to rip his fucking head off.'

I completely understood where he was coming from...I wanted to stick Archie's dick in a food blender but we had to be the bigger people. We had to remain composed, cold and clinical. There was nothing to be gained from shouting, it wasn't going to change anything and would probably just allow them to justify their cheating on us. We entered the hotel and made our way up to room 214. The hotel was unbelievably sumptuous, the décor looked very expensive and I don't think I'd ever seen so many crystal chandeliers. Archie was certainly treating her like the princess she quite clearly thought she was.

We stood outside their room, neither of us knowing what to do next. Ryan actually took the initiative and knocked on the door whilst desperately trying to disguise his voice;

'Delivery for Camilla.'

Ryan's delivery man was clearly someone doing a really bad cockney accent and I worried that he'd blown our cover. I needn't have worried for long as we soon heard Camilla's dulcet tones emanate from behind the closed door;

'Coming sweetie.'

I couldn't fucking believe it...she was flirting with an imaginary delivery man from behind a closed door. My heart started to beat faster as I saw the door handle begin to move. Ryan gripped my hand tightly as it slowly opened to reveal Miss Fucking Perfection Personified wrapped in a bed sheet.

There was a shocked silence as we looked at each other, her expressionless face giving nothing away;

'Who's at the door darling?'

'Darling' What a fucking twat.

'No one special Archie, just your wife and my husband.'

Jesus, that woman was cold...we meant nothing to her. She showed no emotion but a lot of arse as she turned from us and walked back into the room. I could hear Archie scrambling out of bed and he looked dishevelled as he ran to the door in his very expensive complimentary dressing gown;

'Ann, Ryan...I'm so sorry, you shouldn't have had to find out like this.'

Camilla sat on the bed with not an ounce of remorse...to be honest if she wasn't botoxed to the hilt and her face was more expressive you would say she looked like the cat the had got the cream;

'Leave them Archie...at least they know now and we can be together properly.'

The evil bitch...she had destroyed two families and she wasn't even sorry. Who the actual fuck did she think she was? Why, oh fucking why had she always been sitting at my shoulder waiting to pounce on my happiness. The red mist descended and I flew into the hotel room, just by the door was a sweet trolley piled high with cake, fruit and an open bottle of champagne...I'd always wanted a sweet trolley, that should have been mine but she stole it like she stole everything else from me. I grabbed the first thing I could lay my hands on, a beautiful looking strawberry pavlova filled to the brim with fresh cream and I launched it at Camilla's face...yes, direct hit! Oh the satisfaction of seeing her perfectly sculpted face covered in cream. Before I knew it I was grabbing cupcakes and strawberries like a woman possessed and launching them at both Camilla and Archie;

'You want to have your cake and eat it, well here you fucking go.'

I finish of by grabbing the Champagne bottle shaking it for all I was worth and pointing it at the both of them. I was like a woman possessed and I looked on in glee as they stood rooted to the spot. Ryan eventually pulled my back, thankfully he had become calm enough for both of us.

'Remember what you said Ann...they really aren't worth it.'

I looked at Camilla drenched in champagne, covered in cream and cake crumbs. Her fake tan had begun to run and her hair extensions hung limply over her shoulders and I began to cry. She looked a mess, pathetic even, but it was no victory. I turned to leave the room and caught Archie's eye as he took hold of Camilla's hand and gently wiped her cream sodden face. In that moment I knew my marriage was over and Archie...my Dr Gorgeous...was just like every other man I had ever met. When I got home I put all of his belongings into black bin bags and dumped them in the front garden. I had hoped he would at least try and talk to me when he returned but he didn't, he loaded up his car in silence and left to start his new life with that fucking awful woman. In the space of just a few hours my life had been turned upside down...I was Ann with without the 'e' and without my husband.

So here we are six months later. Archie is still with Camilla and Ryan and I are still picking up the pieces. Jude was mortified...not only had his Father left us but he had left us for his best friend's Mum. In his eyes it was the ultimate humiliation and he refused to speak to Archie for the first three months. They are only now starting to rebuild their relationship and Jude has made it clear he will see his Dad but he wants absolutely nothing to do with Camilla. Lola has been a massive support not only to Ryan but also to Jude...she clearly didn't get her personality, empathy and kind heart from her Mother. My friends have also been brilliantly supportive and have now decided I need to get back on the dating horse but, to be honest, I can't be arsed. How on earth do you meet someone when you are a lady of a certain age? Will I have to join a dating site for the over fifties? I bet that's a barrel of fucking laughs. It would be like Stanley all over again except this time it's really my age demographic...I still have visions of his false teeth chattering as he leered at me excitedly. Maybe it's a bit too soon after splitting up with Archie but I certainly don't feel like I want to share my life with another man again. Could I still be an erotic Goddess at age fifty? Am I too old for a good hard shag and a handshake in the morning? Can I still do seductive or when I pout do I look like I'm sucking a lemon and...the biggest question of all...can my fanny still tingle? It's been that fucking long since she's had any attention, I think she's given up, shut up shop and left the building. So that's that then...I need to put on my big girl, or should that be old lady, pants and get back out into the world of dating. Sylvia is coming to see me later so I'm sure she'll be able to give me some advice...if a flamingo mask-wearing, dogging-loving, septuagenarian can't point me in the right direction I'm truly fucked.

CHAPTER TWO

Sylvia's cunning plan

When Archie left the first thing I did was to call my Mum and Dad...it doesn't matter how old you are, when it all goes tits up you turn to your parents. My Dad was naturally furious and if he could have picked up a head of steam in his Zimmer frame, I'm sure he would have gone to confront Archie. He was so lovely, full of concern for me and Jude. As for my Mum, I knew exactly what she would say and when I eventually told her I was spot on;

'You can't give up on him Ann. He's under a lot of stress at work, what with him being a Consultant. Surely you won't give up on your marriage because he made one little mistake.'

'Mum, it was more than a 'little mistake'...he's been shagging Camilla for months. Once is a mistake, three times a night is a fucking travesty!'

'I'm sure he didn't mean it, Ann.'

'He didn't mean it? He didn't mean to spend nights away, he didn't mean to buy her expensive gifts, he didn't mean to let his cock do the talking? For fuck's sake Mother.'

She really didn't want to hear it, she gave me a bollocking for swearing but as far Archie was concerned it was a blip and the sooner I forgave him, the sooner he would be home. Even now six months on he's still 'Saint Archie' and she's still clinging on to the hope we'll get back together...she's going to have a long fucking wait. Archie and I do talk...we have to because of Jude but any love has long gone and we are pretty much like strangers. I'm polite because I want to show that I'm better than him but it's fucking hard believe me.

Sylvia, however, has been my rock these past few months. As soon as I told her what Archie had done she raced over with Adrian. Can you believe they are still together? A year after they met they actually got married and have been sickeningly happy ever since. She's well into her seventies now but you would never think it, she doesn't look that much older than Adrian. I don't know what her secret is but I suspect it's got something to do with the copious amounts of sex she has...with and without the flamingo mask. They were wonderful on that fateful day. Sylvia had the tissues and Prosecco to hand and Adrian took Jude out so he didn't have to see me cry. Adrian has really grown up over the years. Sylvia was good for him...don't get me wrong, he can still be a twat but a more mature, adult one. After she left me she got straight on the phone to Archie. I don't know what she said to him but I truly do believe she 'ripped him a new one'. Although she retired years ago Sylvia still gets invites to functions at the hospital. She has been such a great source of information on Archie and Camilla...it's not that I'm bothered but it fills me with curiosity when she tells me she saw them at an event. Call me bitter and twisted but it does make me laugh when she tells me Camilla looked all pouty, bored and disinterested, whilst Archie looks on in horror as she flirts with anything in a pair of trousers...you always get what you deserve Archiewoowoo.

I feel a little frisson of excitement as she knocks on the door. Apparently she has something to tell me...I do hope Camilla has been caught in flagrante with a handsome younger man...that would teach Archie. Okay so maybe I am a little bit bitter and twisted but can you blame me? I let Sylvia in and we head to the kitchen where I have her favourite tipple waiting. Black tea, no sugar. If she wasn't such a good friend I'm not sure I could forgive her that...who on earth drinks tea with no milk or sugar? It's sacrilege. She makes herself comfortable as I wait with bated breath;

'Sorry I was a bit late Ann. I overslept, Adrian had me up most of the night. My joints have been playing me up a bit recently so he bought me a sex swing and we had to try it out.'

I've heard it all now and really do not want to imagine Sylvia and Adrian in the throes of passion whilst hanging from the bedroom ceiling. In an attempt to change the subject I mention my own joints have been a bit achy recently but due to my menopause rather than shitload of sex;

'Bloody hell, Ann. Have you not been to see your GP yet? There's so much that can be done for you. Get yourself online, there's plenty of really interesting menopause pages to look at...have you considered menopause yoga? It's not the 1950's any more...I bet you refer to it as 'the change' don't you?

'Well, yes I do and I think it's a shit way to describe the menopause, but that's what my Mum always used to call it.'

'What do you think you are going to change into Ann, how do you think your life is going to change? Get yourself sorted or I'll drag you to see the doctor myself.'

  I quickly manage to change the subject (what the hell is menopause yoga?) and promise myself that I will do some research and I will make an appointment. It's just been so full on recently, I feel like I haven't had a minute to myself;

'So come on Sylvia. You said you had something exciting to tell me...what is it? Has she dumped Archie for a younger, richer, model? Has he dumped her for a younger, richer model? Are they staying together but getting matching arse implants?..tell me!'

'I've got you a date, Ann.'

She's fucking what now? What was she thinking? I know, I said I was up for getting back on the dating scene but this is too soon. I've changed my mind. On reflection I don't want to go on a date...I don't want to go near another man, ever. Maybe a nunnery is a good idea at this stage in my life or perhaps I could go off somewhere spiritual to find myself...the one thing I do know is that a man is a definite no no. My heart is not available and my bearded clam snapped shut the day Archie left.

'It's very kind of you to think about me Sylvia but I'm not ready to go on a date just yet.'

'So when are you going to be ready...tomorrow, next week, next year. You were all enthusiastic about dating the other day...what happened?'

'Nothing happened. I just thought about it again and decided that dating is not for me...not any more.'

'Well that's just silly, Ann. You are a beautiful, intelligent, funny woman. Why would you stop living because of the selfish, vain twat you just happened to marry.'

'Because he just happened to break my heart into a million pieces and I'm not putting myself through that again.'

'Listen. You know that I understand. How many years did I shun dating for? All those years when I could have been happy. If I'd carried on thinking the way you are now, I never would have met Adrian. I would still be having random anonymous sex hidden behind a mask rather than swinging from the ceiling with my gorgeous hunk of a husband.'

She did have a point I suppose. Maybe it would do me good to get out and about. If Archie is having the time of his life why shouldn't I?

'Go on then, tell me about him and I'll think about it.'

'Well I met him at a charity function I went to a couple of days ago. He's just moved back to the area after a rather painful divorce. He's a banker for the group that was funding the event. He's gorgeous Ann...about your age, tall and lean with the most amazing blue eyes and a really hypnotic smile. I told him all about you and he's keen to meet up...a blind date Ann, how exciting.'

I have to admit he did sound rather nice and rather familiar. I couldn't quite put my finger on it but he definitely sounded like some one I knew.

'What's his name Sylvia?'

'His name is Daniel and he was delectable.'

Oh for fuck's sake she's taking the piss now...the delectable Daniel!?

'I can't Sylvia...I really can't. I think that's 'the' Daniel. Remember I told you about him. I spilt red hot wax on his dick. I know it was a long time ago but I'm guessing you don't forget something like that...oh shit, and then when I saw him again not that long after, I let him believe Stanley was my Dad so I could sit in the car with him...it's not happening.'

Once Sylvia stopped laughing she explained that he had asked quite a lot of questions about me, one being 'does she like scented candles?' So he obviously thought I sounded familiar...which means he hadn't forgotten about me. Is that a good thing or a bad thing? I couldn't, could I? I must admit the thought of seeing him again was a little intriguing...not intriguing enough to make my fanny tingle but it could be fun.

'Oh, Sylvia, I can't decide...should I?'

'Of course you should! It might be fun and, you never know, you might be able to get another wax souvenir to replace the one you lost. If nothing else you'll have a laugh and you could really do with a laugh right now...all that frowning isn't good for your wrinkles. I took the liberty of arranging a time and date for you.'

'Right, I'll do it...you,re right it could be fun and I can't wait to see what Daniel looks like now. So when am I meeting him?'

'Tonight.'

'Are you fucking kidding me...tonight?'

'I didn't want to give you the opportunity to change your mind. So you are meeting him outside the Dog and

Partridge at 8pm...no excuses.'

'But what about Jude...I need to ask him if he's okay with me meeting up with someone.'

'Already done. Adrian had a chat with him yesterday and he thinks it's a great idea. Lola is coming round tonight to keep him company.'

The devious shits, they had sorted it all out behind my back...wait until I speak to Adrian.

As I say goodbye to Sylvia my head is spinning. I'm going on a fucking date...with Daniel. I don't even want to try and calculate how many years it's been since I last saw him so I do it in kilograms...it's been twelve kilograms mainly on my arse since I last saw him. Maybe it is destiny. I always said I thought Daniel could have been 'the one'. Perhaps he was 'the one' but it was the wrong time and now fate has randomly thrown us together...I think I seriously need to stop reading the romance again and dig out my erotic novels because I really am talking shit. Right, I need to think about what I am going to wear and I really need to think about what I'm going to say...do I mention the wax bellend incident or just pretend it never happened in the hope he's forever erased it from his memory...what the fuck have I done?

CHAPTER THREE

'Big D'

I'm going on a date with Dan the man...who would have thought it after all these years? Sylvia didn't give me an awful lot of notice, so I just had time for a quick bath and muff trim. Not that she's going to be seeing any action...I'd need pruning shears if I thought a shag was on the cards. As far as I'm concerned it's less a date and more a catch up with an old friend. As we're meeting at the pub, I decide to opt for a casual look, jeans and a fairly cleavage enhancing top. I've got to show these babies off, I've waited long enough to get them. I put my hair up as there's not much else I can do with it these days. My once glossy curls are suffering from my distinct lack of hormones and now resemble a 1970's minge...come to think of it they actually just resemble my minge in its current state. I have another quick look in the mirror before I leave to revisit my past...minus my youth, the sex and a scented candle.

I'm waiting outside the pub for Daniel to arrive and I have to admit, I am absolutely shitting myself. It's been so long since I went on a first date, I've forgotten what to do. I suppose the way to look at it is...it's not actually a first date. It's a second date, albeit nearly two decades after the first one. I wonder whether we'll still have anything in common? As I mulling over some conversation starters, I see a very flashy sports car pull into the car park. I don't know why but something tells me this is going to be him. My heart starts to pound as it parks up and the door opens. It's been a long, long time since I've done this and I feel like a complete novice. He steps out of the car and, oh my goodness, it is him and he is even fitter than I remember him. His face is fuller and he's got a whisper of grey around his temples but that makes him look distinguished. Hang on a minute...what the hell is he wearing? Ripped jeans, a muscle fit top and slip on shoes without socks...for fuck's sake he looks like he's been dressed by Love Island. As he walks towards me alarm bells start to ring. It's all a bit Archie...the youthful clothes, the sports car. I make a mental note to check for a clip on ponytail before things go too far.

To my surprise he seems pleased to see me. He strides purposefully towards me and kisses me on both cheeks...I think I may just have had the beginnings of a fanny tingle;

'Oh my God, Ann. It's so good to see you. You haven't changed a bit. When Sylvia described her friend who would make a fantastic blind date...I knew it was you.'

Well, that sounds promising. I think he could do with a trip to Specsavers but I'll take the compliment. As we head into the pub I make sure to walk behind him and I'm so pleased to say there's no hint of a clip on ponytail so I might be onto something here;

'What would you like to drink...if I remember correctly it's a Prosecco?'

He's remembered what I like to drink...mind you after what I did to him, he's probably never going to forget that night. I really have to address the elephant in the room so as soon as he sits down I open my mouth without engaging my brain;

'I'm still so sorry for what happened, Daniel, and even after all these years, I still don't know what the fuck happened.'

'It's ancient history, like I told you when I took you to the hospital to see your Dad, there was no lasting damage.'

Without even thinking it through I immediately blurt out the truth;

'He wasn't my Dad. He was a date who had lied about his age and I lied about being his daughter so I could get to spend some time with you.'

Why oh why am I such a twat?

'Well that's very flattering...if not a bit stalkery. Tell me what have you been up to?'

Fucking fabulous. Not only does he think I can't let go of the past he also thinks I'm a stalker. I go on to to tell him about my marriage to Archie and the disaster that was Miss Fucking Perfection Personified. He's very sympathetic and it transpires he only ever went on a couple of dates with Camilla, she was too much like hard work apparently. I didn't have the heart to tell him she described him as 'terribly dull'. He is also in the process of getting a divorce...no fault on either side, they had just fallen out of love with each other and become more like friends.

As the evening goes on we are chatting away like old friends. I'm mesmerised by his still sparkly blue eyes and his smile is melting away all the barriers I'd surrounded myself with. I think he's flirting with me but it's been so long since I,ve been on a date I'm not sure I'm reading the signals right...he could be or maybe he's just being friendly? The moment I start to wonder whether I should have given my muff a good pruning after all' a group of young women enter the pub. They are all beautiful...so beautiful if they'd been on Instagram you would swear they'd used filters. Daniel is immediately distracted and can't take his eyes off them;

'I'm just going to the bar, Ann...you look like you could do with a top up.'

My glass is still full. I watch as he heads straight for the group of young goddesses and stands right next to them. He immediately starts to make conversation with one them...the most beautiful one. I can see she is dazzled by his smile and she's doing the flirtatious hair flicking thing that I could never quite get right because of my unruly curls. I don't think she can me more that twenty five years old...he's old enough to be her Father. Maybe that's it...he's just taking a fatherly interest. Getting down with the kids in that cringey way Dads do. Well he's been served at the bar so there's no reason for him not to come and sit down. Only he doesn't, he spends another ten minutes chatting away without a thought for me sitting here on my own like Billy no mates. I'm starting to feel impatient and try waving at him...he fucking ignored me! So I wave again and again until he turns his back on me...well I'm not having that! I go to the bar and tap him on the shoulder;

'Daniel...you appear to have forgotten something.'

He looks confused.

'Me, Daniel, you've forgotten me.'

   He apologises to The Beautiful One and whispers something in her ear. Then he ushers me back to our table and raises his eyebrows in exasperation...like he's been saddled with the eccentric, middle aged Aunty at a wedding. We sit down but the conversation has completely died. It really does feel like he doesn't want to be here and after about ten minutes of smiling and nodding politely to each other he gets up;

'Ann, I just need to nip to the car for five minutes...I completely forgot I've got a business email I need to send.'

   With that he heads off to the car park. I don't know what to do with myself so neck back one of my glasses of Prosecco and have a scroll through my phone. Jude has message me to say he hopes I'm having a good time...I"ll just reply 'yes' rather than 'not really...my date has gone all weird on me'. Five minutes passes, then ten and now he's been gone twenty minutes I'm starting to get impatient. Fuck it...I might make me look a bit needy but I'm going to go and find him. Who knows what might have happened to him? I catch sight of his car in the car park but Daniel is nowhere to be seen. I quickly walk over to it and have a look through the window...you never know, he might have fainted or something. But he's definitely not in the car - so where the hell is he? The car park is pretty deserted and I'm just about to go back inside when I hear giggling. I head towards the noise and it takes me to an alley behind the kitchen. I find Daniel, bathed in light from the pub with his tongue so far down The Beautiful One's throat he'll be able to sample what she had for dinner and what the fuck is he doing with his hands? Well that's just fucking marvellous. What an utter twat...he can take his midlife crisis and shove it up his arse. I'm going home. I don't let on that I've seen them...I can't be arsed with a confrontation and I'm too old for all this bullshit. As I walk past his car, my maturity and new found calm fly out of the window. I can't help myself. Fuck it...why should I go quietly? I pull my bright red lipstick out of my bag and write TWAT on his windscreen. Feeling empowered, I turn to walk away but as I do I notice that the window of the pub toilets is right above Daniel and the beautiful one. Suddenly a lipstick smeared twat doesn't seem quite enough, so I go back into the pub and head straight for the bar;

'Could I have a jug of water please with plenty of ice.'

Mission accomplished I climb the stairs and head to the toilets...fuck, this is immature but you don't mess with Ann without the 'e'. I'm menopausal, been around the block a few times and just don't have the patience for this level of fuckwittery. Once in the toilets, I open the window to be greeted with the sound of more inane giggling which soon turns into high pitched screams as I pour the freezing cold contents of the water jug all over them. I leave the jug on the floor and exit the toilets as fast as I can, ducking behind a pillar as I see Daniel and The Beautiful One coming back into the pub. She looks absolutely furious and I'm pissing myself laughing as I hear Daniel trying to placate her;

'I'm sorry babe...I don't know what happened but you still look gorgeous. You look like you've just won a wet t-shirt competition.'

'You look like you've just won a wet t-shirt competition'...for fuck's sake, Daniel. Does he really think that's going to help. She's not old enough to know what a wet t-shirt competition is! The man really has grown his twat wings as he's got older. I don't look back as I sneak out of the pub doors. I should have listened to my inner voice...when was this ever going to be a good idea? I make a mental note never to let Sylvia arrange a date for me again. Daniel was never my destiny especially not in those jeans.

As soon as I get home Jude and Lola want to know how I got on...what do I say;

'Daniel was still fit but looked like a bit of a knob in his ripped jeans.'

'I thought I was well in until he binned me off for some bird half my age.'

'Unfortunately my knickers are too large and comfortable for him to try and get into.'

I settle on telling them he was called away on urgent business...he urgently needed both his ego and his cock massaging. My first date in what feels like a lifetime and he bins me off within the hour for a younger model...what a fucking travesty. As I pour myself a drink my phone pings with a message;

'Hey Ann. What happened to you? I had a bit of an accident with some water and when I got back to the table and you had gone. Did you see anyone suspicious when you left? Someone scrawled twat all over my windscreen.'

Cheeky bastard...what happened Daniel was the minute

you had your head turned you didn't give me a second thought. I can't really be arsed responding but I suppose I'd better let him know I'm alright;

'Sorry I didn't get to say goodbye but when I came outside to find you, you looked rather busy with your new friend. Clearly, I didn't want to interrupt you mid wank so I thought I'd just slip off home. I do hope nothing happened to dampen your evening.'

He gets back to me straight away;

'Oh yes. Sorry about that. Hang on...the water, the 'twat', was that you?

'No Daniel... the 'twat' was you.'

Not surprisingly he doesn't message me back. He gave me an hour of his time and then he was off, clearly he saw me as no more than an old friend with the emphasis being on the old. I'm so disappointed, not because the date didn't work out but because he was every stereotype of a middle aged man...just like Archie. I bet he knocks twenty years of his age and refers to himself as 'Big D' or 'The D Man'. If older men only like women half their age then I think I'd better get myself a job in a nursing home as it's the only way I'll get to meet someone in the age group that would be interested in me. So it's pretty conclusive...Daniel is definitely not my destiny but being out was fun and maybe now is the time to start dating again. I'm not interested in finding Mr Uninhibited or Mr Romance, Mr I Won't Sack You Off For A Younger Model will do me just fine. I'll sleep on it and decide once and for all in the morning.

CHAPTER FOUR

Back in the dating game

I had a restless night's sleep, not only did I have lot to think about but since I plunged headlong into the menopause my brain just won't switch off and my sleep has been stupidly disturbed. I either barely get to sleep at all or if I do, no matter what time I go to bed I'm woken up by the menopause fairy at 5am. I really must make that doctor's appointment. I can't remember the last time I woke up in the morning feeling refreshed and without stiff joints and because I'm busy and keep putting the doctor off, I spent the night wide awake still sniggering at the look on Daniel's face as he desperately tried to calm The Beautiful One down. The vision of him struggling to follow her at pace in his too tight jeans whilst calling out 'babe' will stay with me forever. He really was fighting with every inch of his life to maintain his midlife dream and I can't help wondering whether they exchanged phone numbers at the end of the night, did 'Big D' get his much sought after younger woman or did he go home alone to a cup of cocoa? When I wasn't laughing, I was going backwards and forwards through the pros and cons of dating again.

Pros

I could do with some adult male company. As much as I love spending time with my son, it's just not right that a woman of my age knows so much about PlayStation games.

I deserve a bit of happiness. I'm in the prime of my life and I have so much living to do...fuck the fuckers. I'm my own woman and I'll dictate my own destiny.

I'm well overdue some non battery operated fanny tingles.

Cons

What if I get let down again? I still feel so hurt and betrayed by Archie. Lets face it, I'm not exactly known for my luck when it comes to men.

So...the pros outweigh the cons and the only thing that is holding me back is the fear of being let down again. I need to seize the day, remember who I am...Ann without the 'e' ageing erotic goddess with a cracking pair of tits. I don't need to get tips from erotic literature any more because what I lack in youth, I more then make up for in experience. I think I've made my decision...I'm going to go for it. Nothing ventured nothing gained and if I don't try I'll never know. I have to go to a concert at Jude's school this afternoon but I think I'll just have enough time to set the wheels in motion and start my brand new dating adventure...if I don't do it now, I never will.

I've done a bit or research online and as much as I said I never would, I'm going to sign up for an over fifties dating site. Surely it won't be that bad? aAfter all fifty is the new thirty or is it the new twenty?..I can never remember. I've reasoned that if I join a more mature site,

I'll be sure that my potential date won't be wearing ripped jeans and a shirt unbuttoned down to his navel and if he does, I know I need to run a mile. After a lot of searching, I eventually find a site that looks suitable and upload my details...my profile is a little half hearted and my picture is, shall we say, an honest representation of my lines and menopausal minge hair. I'm in two minds whether to post it or not when I remember my mantra from my early dating days...I am what I am and if it's not good enough they can fuck off. I click done and my dating fate is now in the hands of the Gods...I must admit it is a little exciting. This could be the start of something fabulous, the beginning of a brand new chapter in my life. I'm going to be swept off my feet by my very own knight on a white charger. Just as I'm getting wrapped up in my very own romantic fantasy my phone pings. It's a dick pic, closely followed by another and then a dick and balls shot...Oh dear, his bollocks are hanging down to his knees. I knew this was a bad idea...I wanted to be wooed not bombarded with elderly knobs. They remind me of turkey necks without the gobbling...I just couldn't. I didn't think there was much that could shock me at my age but for fuck's sake...dick pics in middle age, surely they are having a laugh? I naively thought that older men would have left the dick pic phase behind them...men clearly never mature and I clearly still have a lot to learn.

After the initial flurry of foreskin my phone finally pings with a real message. It's from Doug and he actually looks quite nice, he's asking me to take a look at his profile so of course I'll have to oblige. He's a serial entrepreneur and investor which probably means he owns a couple of burger places on the seafront...I may have become more cynical with age. He's 51 and has never been married or had children. Completely uncomplicated...that has to be a bonus. Doug is starting to look like a prospect until I read what he is looking for in a date;

'I am looking for a long term relationship. I am an affluent businessman who eats at the best restaurants and travels abroad four to five times a year. I am looking for a lady to share these experiences with me. However, if you want to be my lady you have to act like one. I cannot tolerate swearing or the expulsion of any bodily noises. You must dress like a lady...no jeans, trainers or bomber jackets. You must be available at short notice to attend functions where you will be required to behave impeccably...when out with me you are my representative and your behaviour should reflect this. You must have the ability to prepare food to the highest standard and keep your house in good order, I do not like mess. A messy house means a messy brain and my lady must be on the ball at all times. You should not have small children, I made the decision to remain childless and do not wish to be in the company of children. Older teenagers are acceptable as long as I don't have to interact with them in any way. If you can comply to all my requests please feel free to message me back.'

That has to be a joke...there's no way that can be real, can it? I message him back immediately;

'Hi Doug, love your profile. You obviously have a really good sense of humour.'

'Thanks for getting back to me, Ann. Though I'm not sure why you think I'm joking.'

What the fuck...it's real!

'Thanks for clarifying your profile is real. How long have you been single for?'

He obviously thinks he's onto something as my phone pings with his reply straight away.

'I can't remember exactly but I think it's about ten years now. Most of my dates haven't lasted beyond the first one.'

Is he fucking surprised?

'Doug...have you ever wondered why that might be? Maybe your standards are a little too high. I'm clearly not for you. I swear like a fucking trooper, I can burp the alphabet and I'm not adverse to farting on a first date. I wear what I want, not what is required of me and I'm a rubbish cook with a house which is lived in and therefore usually quite messy. I behave how I want. I represent myself so if you think you can deal with dating a middle aged, menopausal woman who doesn't have the patience to deal with fuckwits then please message me back.'

Not surprisingly he doesn't get back to me. What a complete and utter wanker. Who in their right mind would comply to those demands? I'm wondering whether this was a good idea. All I've attracted so far is dick pics and an actual dick. Maybe this dating in your fifties business isn't going to be as easy as I thought.

I put all thoughts of dating out of my head as I get ready to go to Jude's concert. This was going to be the first time I would see Archie and the delightful Camilla together since that day in the hotel. Obviously I've had to speak to Archie since as we have Jude to consider. It's always been very polite and, although every time I see him I have the urge to knee him in the bollocks, I've always managed to keep my cool. He's still not given me an explanation as to why he betrayed me. He's apologised but not given me any reason other than 'it was one of those things, people fall out of love all the time.' Well I don't fall out of love all the time, you fickle twat. How could I have been so wrong about someone? I would have bet my house on Archie being faithful until the end of our days together but then Miss Fucking Perfection Personified came along. What the fuck do they see in that woman? Yes, she's very attractive but the woman has no fucking soul, she's so shallow she makes a puddle look deep. I can feel my eyes start to fill with tears and give myself a kick. Today is about Jude. I'm not going to shed another tear over that man nor am I going to give that awful woman the satisfaction of knowing I'm upset. She probably bathes in the tears of women she's fucked over...that must be what keeps her young.

I'm sitting alone in the school hall waiting for the concert to start when Archie and Camilla arrive. Camilla's now humongous breasts enter the hall a couple of seconds before the rest of her body, her teeth are even whiter and her lips are even more plumped. She's becoming a caricature of herself but clearly doesn't give a shit as she looks like the cat that got the cream. This is their first outing to school together and she clearly wants everyone to know about her new catch. One of the Mums sitting behind me gently pats my shoulder as Archie and Camilla sit down right in front of me. Archie turns around and nods in acknowledgement of my presence. Miss Fucking Perfection Personified ignores me completely. Fuck the fuckers...I'm here for my son. The concert starts and it's not long before Camilla becomes bored with listening to off-key teenagers sing the latest chart hits; she gets out her phone and is tapping away furiously as every other parent in the room claps and cheers. Before long it's Jude and Lola's turn to perform. Jude plays the piano as Lola sings along...they are brilliant. I don't know where he gets his musical talent from...it must be his Father who has become quite adept at playing old tunes on a new piano. When they finish both Archie and I jump to our feet and begin to clap. The evil one doesn't even look up from her phone. I notice Archie give her a gentle nudge but she ignores him and carries on...what could be so important it makes you ignore your child's amazing achievement?

Concert over, the parents are chatting over a cup of tea and a ginger nut biscuit. I keep my head down and my distance the last thing I want is a confrontation. Archie is deep in conversation with Jude's head of year when Camilla strides purposefully across the hall;

'Come on now Archie...I've got a last minute appointment for a colonic irrigation and if we don't go now, I'm going to be late.'

A colonic what now? A couple of parents simultaneously spit their tea out and Archie doesn't know where to look. He shrugs his shoulders in resignation and follows her out of the room like lost sheep. Archie now looks like Ryan did all those years ago...absolutely broken. He has alienated almost everyone close to him over that dreadful woman. Sylvia thought of him like a son but now can barely look at him and his own Mother is mortified. Although she disapproved of me when she first met me, we have become incredibly close over the years and the support she has given me and Jude since

Archie left has been amazing. She cannot understand why Archie would break up our family for that 'awful woman.' The only person in our circle that hasn't turned their back on him is my Mum...cheers for the loyalty Mum. I had hoped that once she got used to the idea she would accept he'd been a twat and move on but, ever the social climber, she's clinging onto her Mother in Law of a doctor credentials for as long as she can. Once Archie and Camilla have left I say my goodbyes to Jude and Lola and decide to sneak out of the door at the back of the hall. I can't bear one more sympathetic look...it's lovely that people care, I just don't want to be reminded what a fuck up my life is. I wave to Jude and he's mouthing something as I'm about to pull the door handle down...it looks like 'no' but I can't make it out. He's probably saying 'love you' so I mouth it back as I open the door. As I bring the handle down the loudest alarm goes off. I think I pee a little with the shock and then it hits me...I opened the fire exit and set the fire alarms off. Oh for fuck's, fucking sake. I can't be trusted anywhere. Rather than be the mature woman I am and admit my mistake, I leg it. As I run towards the road, I look back to see a stream of pupils exiting the school...I can never go back.

I'm feeling hot, sweaty and anxious by the time I get home. I'm not sure whether to blame my hormones or my own stupidity...I decide it's a combination of both. What was I thinking? Just as I'm despairing in myself I get a message from Jude;

'Great move, Mum. You setting the fire alarm off got us out of physics. My mates think you're top.'

Well at least someone is happy...and rather than being a walking disaster, I'm now regarded as a 'cool' Mum. Just as I finally compose myself my phone pings with a message again. It's from the dating site and thankfully it's not an aged knob of any variety. The message is from Frank...he's 50 like me, divorced with two children and he looks well fit. I quickly check out his full profile and I'm thrilled to say he's not making any outrageous demands. This is rather exciting, Frank could be a prospect.

CHAPTER FIVE

Frank

I'm meeting Frank shortly and I have to admit I do feel a bit anxious. I'm not counting the Daniel disaster as a date, so this is my first date in more years than I care to remember. What if I've forgotten what to do? We've exchanged a few messages over the past few days and although I wouldn't say he was exactly chatty he does come across as rather sweet. Maybe that's where I've gone wrong over the years. I've always been attracted to dynamic men, perhaps I need to be looking for someone more reserved. It's not taken me too long to get ready. I've dressed casually again as I'm meeting him in the Dog and Partridge...it's like Groundhog Day and I'm starting to wonder whether dating in middle age will ever deviate from meeting up for a quick half in the local boozer. I've had to straighten my hair as it's frizzier than ever and I've tidied up my rather unruly eyebrows...I was channelling my inner Bert from Sesame Street before I plucked them. I have quick look in the mirror before I leave and I'm happy with the result...until I see the longest, thickest black hair making its presence known on my chin. I swear that fucker wasn't there yesterday when I did my daily pluck...the bastards seem to appear overnight just to remind me I've reached that certain age. I search everywhere for my tweezers and they are nowhere to be seen. Where the fuck are they? I can't go out looking like Catweazle. In desperation,I have a look through Archie's tool box and end up plucking it out with a pair of pliers...job done.

It's raining so I've arranged to meet Frank inside. I've learnt over the years that freshly straightened hair should not be exposed to moisture under any circumstances. He should remember what I look like from my picture but just to be sure he finds me, I told him I would be wearing a red top. I get myself a glass of Prosecco and find a seat. Almost as soon as I sit down I see Frank enter the pub...he's punctual at least. He's tall, tanned and ruggedly handsome, his ice blue eyes are staring at me intently as he walks over clutching the most beautiful bunch of flowers...happy days!

'Hi, Ann, so pleased to meet you. These are for you.'

I suddenly forget I'm a fifty year old woman of experience and giggle coquettishly like I'm on my first ever date;

'Thank you so much,Frank, it's been a long time since anyone bought me flowers.'

'My pleasure, beautiful flowers for a beautiful lady.'

I think I'm blushing and I'm suddenly filled with enthusiasm about my new found single status, especially when without a word, Frank heads straight to the bar and brings me back a bottle of Prosecco. I don't have the heart to tell him there's no way I'll be able to drink it all. As I've got older my capacity for alcohol has diminished...more than two glasses and I'm doing karaoke and back flipping off bar stools. As I thought from our messages, Frank is a little quiet and the conversation is a bit stilted. He seems quite content nursing his pint and although I'm more than happy to stare into his beautiful blue eyes, it's starting to get a bit awkward. Each time there's a pregnant pause in the conversation I take a large gulp of my drink...I need to slow down a bit and I really need to get the conversation flowing;

'So tell me about yourself Frank. I'm pretty unremarkable really. I'm divorced and have one lovely son. This is the first proper date I've been on since I split from my husband what about you?'

He pauses, takes a deep breath and I immediately regret asking him;

'It's been a year since my divorce came through and I've only been on a couple of dates since. I just haven't had the heart. I haven't wanted to see anyone to be honest. I was married for thirty years. My wife was all I had ever known but she fell out of love with me. I admit I've found it difficult to move on, whereas she's shacked up with some bloke from work and looks happier than ever. No one could ever compare to her...she was my everything. You remind me so much of her, especially in that top...she really suited red, too. She was slimmer than you especially around the bottom but as soon as I saw your profile I knew I had to meet you because you could be her.'

I neck my drink in one. What the fuck? Not only is he saying I've got a big arse, he's only dating me because I remind him of his wife...I'm his wife substitute! It's also a little strange he refers to her as his wife in the present tense...not his 'ex' or 'ex-wife.' The sensible part of my brain thinks now would be a good time to leave but the soft part of it feels really sorry for him. He's clearly had his heart broken into tiny pieces and at least he has a heart which is a good start. I decide to take control of the situation and talk about anything and everything to distract him from his marital woes. I try to encourage him to talk about his hobbies, what's on telly and even 'what colour is your favourite fruit pastille.' I find out he likes the red ones but I also know that his wife liked knitting, Coronation Street and Leonardo DiCaprio.   I've been knocking back the Prosecco and I'm starting to feel rather pissed...can you blame me? I feel like I'm on a date from the Twilight Zone. Finally Frank speaks first and asks me if I would like something to eat. I enthusiastically agree, a bit of food might soak up some of the alcohol. I don't think anyone in the pub is ready for my rendition of 'I am what I am' just yet.

I've ordered the grilled courgette. I would have loved a burger or a steak but I'm trying to improve my diet now I'm menopausal. I did actually go online and do some research...Sylvia will be so proud and if it improves my health and gets her off my back it's well worth it. I'm absolutely starving and rather shitfaced by the time the food arrives. I look on enviously as Frank's steak arrives and when the waiter puts my plate in front of me it takes me a moment to register what I see on my plate. To my amusement, I find myself starting at one long, limp grilled courgette and unfortunately the first thing that comes into my mind comes out of my mouth;

'Oh my God, it looks like a cock.'

If that wasn't bad enough, I feel compelled to stick my fork into it and wave it around whilst describing its cock-like features. The table behind us is laughing hysterically, the table next to us not so much and Frank clearly doesn't know where to put himself. As the waiter starts to approach our table, I sense he might be about to give me a bollocking so I quickly drop the courgette back onto the plate and suddenly feel like that eccentric aunty at a wedding. My bad behaviour at least prompts Frank to speak;

'My wife would never have done that.'

Oh not the wife again...this is the first date I've been on in over a decade and he won't stop talking about her. I really don't know what the fuck he's doing here;

'I'm not your wife, Frank.'

Maybe that was a bit too blunt as he looks mortified and against my better judgement, I take another large sip of my drink. We pretty much sit in silence as we eat our pudding, however this is not a bad thing as woe betide anyone who comes between me and chocolate profiteroles. Just as I think I've totally fucked the evening up, Frank surprises me;

'I'd love to see you again, Ann.'

I have to ask him to repeat himself because I'm sure he just said he'd like to see me again. I feel a bit confused. I thought I'd totally ballsed up the whole evening. What the fuck should I do? He is rather handsome but he's devoid of personality and clearly not over his wife. Maybe he'd be more animated next time and perhaps I could help mend his broken heart. Once again my alcohol fuelled mouth speaks before I can think everything through logically;

'Yes Frank, it would be great to meet up again.'

He smiles and gently touches my hand...could that be a fanny tingle I can feel or am I just sitting awkwardly?

We pay the bill and leave the pub through the back doors and into the car park. Once we are outside Frank stops me;

'I've really enjoyed this evening, Ann. Would you mind if I kissed you?'

What a gentleman...do I mind if he kisses me? Do I fuck! I lean in and he kisses me passionately which to be honest is a surprise. He's been so quiet all evening I was expecting a quick peck on the lips. Frank is a really great kisser and I'm starting to wonder what else he could do so well. I pull him into the alley where I saw Daniel and The Beautiful One and kiss him again. It's been such a long time since I've kissed anyone and it feels good. I slip my hand inside his trousers and his cock is hard, I gently grasp it and suddenly a thought pops into my head...Frank rhymes with wank. I can't help myself and I start to laugh. He pulls away and looks crushed;

'It's okay, Ann...my wife used to laugh as well.'

I feel fucking awful;

'No Frank...I'm not laughing at your penis, it felt like a very nice penis. I just thought Frank rhymes with wank and considering what I was just about to do, it made me laugh.'

'It felt like a very nice penis?' I'm never drinking again. Frank doesn't look convinced;

'It's been a lovely evening Ann but I don't think we should see each other again. Maybe you are too much like my wife for it ever work.'

I try to explain again but he's having no of it. He walks off without a second glance and yet again I find myself on my own...what a complete and utter disaster.

My head is spinning in the taxi on the way home. How

did I let myself get into this state? I know I can't drink much but I still did...I'm a complete twat. After some fumbling around for my keys, I manage to let myself into my house. I'm trying to be as quiet as possible which isn't easy when you can barely walk in a straight line. I think I've managed to sneak past Jude who's playing on his games console but just as I pass the door;

'Night Mum, hope you had a good night and don't forget to drink plenty of water.'

  Shit, can he tell I'm pissed? I feel like I'm the wayward teenager who's home by ten but hammered because they've been drinking cider in the bus shelter behind the bowling green and he's the adult...tonight is turning into one embarrassment after another. Poor Frank, I think I may have destroyed the little bit of self-confidence he had left. I fire him off a quick message to apologise again for the misunderstanding but I'm not expecting to hear back from him. I do hope he manages to move on from his marriage, everyone deserves to be happy...well everyone apart from Miss Fucking Perfection

Personified. I think she's done a deal with the devil so she remains happy no matter what she does or who she hurts.

I get a glass of water and head up to bed feeling deflated and secure in the knowledge my head was really going to hurt in the morning. My phone is full of messages but I'm not looking until the morning if I look now, I'd probably tell the dick pic I'd love to meet him and the man of my dreams to fuck off. I drift off to sleep quickly but it lasts no longer than a couple of hours. I can hear my phone ringing and wonder whether I'm dreaming. I pick up and it's my cousin Adrian...it's not a dream but a nightmare;

'Ann you need to come round, Sylvia has had a fall and she won't let me get any help.'

I fly out of bed and throw some clothes on. Luckily Sylvia and Adrian only live around the corner so it won't take me long to get to them. I tell Jude where I'm going and run as fast as my still ever so slightly pissed legs will carry me. I knock on the door and Adrian answers...he's wearing the tiniest of tiny thongs, my poor eyes are never going to unsee that and I'm sick in my mouth a little;

'For fuck's sake Adrian, could you not have put some clothes on? Where's Sylvia and what happened?'

'She's upstairs in our bedroom. We were gearing up for a night of passion and she slipped getting into the sex swing. She's on the floor and I can't move her.'

I push past Adrian to get upstairs, there's no way I want to follow him and see the back view...my stomach wouldn't cope. I open the door to the bedroom and the shocks just keep on coming. Sylvia is stark bollock naked. I don't know where to look so I grab the quilt off the bed and cover her up as I go in;

'What have you done Sylvia? We really need to get you to hospital.'

'I think I've broken my hip. I'm a doctor, remember, and I know that at my age once you start going into hospital its a slippery slope...I'm not ready for a care home just yet.'

'Oh for fuck's sake, Sylvia. You will never end up in a care home...you'll probably outlive all of us. You must get your hip checked out, what else are you going to do...lie on the floor until you do die?I'm calling an ambulance whether you like it or not.'

Sylvia tries to protest but I'm having none of it. I'm not ready to lose Sylvia and if me calling an ambulance pisses her off than so be it.

Thankfully we don't have to wait too long for the ambulance to arrive and Sylvia flirts outrageously with the the two young, male paramedics...this is a good sign, if Sylvia was quiet in the presence of handsome young men, I would be worried. Adrian goes with her in the ambulance and I follow on foot, the fresh air is doing wonders for my hangover. I arrive at the hospital and head straight for A&E. I don't need to ask where Sylvia is...I can hear her;

'Listen to me...I don't need to see a consultant, just send me down for an x-ray and then I can get out of here.'

Sylvia is clearly going to be the patient from hell. I walk into the cubicle and Adrian is dutifully trying to hold her hand...she's having none of it and keeps brushing him away. It all looks very awkward so as soon as I walk in, I tell Adrian to go and get us all a coffee. As he leaves, Sylvia looks relieved;

'Thanks for that, Ann. He's trying his best but to be honest he's really getting on my tits. I just want to go home but I've got to wait for the consultant. I told them I was practising medicine when their consultant was a twinkle in his Father's eye but they are not listening and I don't know anyone who is on tonight.'

She's starting to get stressed so I tell her I'll go and find out where the consultant is. I don't have to wait too long, as soon as I draw the curtain back I find myself face to face with him...it's Archie. Oh fuck, what do I say, what do I do? I find myself looking him straight in his eyes and I'm taken right back to the first time we met. Only I don't have any fanny tingles just a deep feeling of sadness. Archie looks taken aback to see me, he should have known I would be with Sylvia. He mutters a greeting and walks straight past me to talk to Sylvia. I don't know what he says to her as my head is all over the place and all I can hear is noise. He pops his head out of the curtain and calls for a porter to take her for an x-ray. Sylvia mouths an apology as she leaves the room but Archie stays put. Once she's gone he draws the curtain and I'm feeling slightly confused;

'Ann, I'm so pleased to see you. I really need to talk to you.'

What on earth would he want to talk to me about? There's nothing outstanding with Jude and the solicitor has everything he needs for the divorce. Maybe he's dumped Camilla and wants to come home, he did look awfully pissed off at the school concert...what would I do? I couldn't take him back after everything. Could I?

'It's about me and Camilla.'

Here we go. He's realised she's a high maintenance, blood sucking twat from hell and he unceremoniously dumped her when she got home from her colonic irrigation.

'I've asked her to marry me.'

He's what now? I thought he just said he's asked Miss Fucking Perfection Personified to marry him.

'So I need to speed the divorce up...Camilla has her heart set on a summer wedding in the Caribbean.'

I am actually speechless. This isn't the Archie I first met. When did he become so cold and heartless, he's speaking to me as if I'm an inconvenience. In that one moment any love I had left for him died.

'Archie. If you think I'm going to speak to my solicitor to rush the divorce through so you can marry that feckless trollop you are fucking insane. Is it even wise for her to go somewhere as hot as the Caribbean?..she's so plastic she might just melt. I'm sorry Archie but I would rather eat my own eyeballs than make it easy for you. Not because I'm harbouring thoughts of you coming home but because you are behaving like an complete and utter cunt. It's like all those years we spent together and our son mean nothing to you.'

'Come on Ann, you know Jude means the world to me.'

  Well, that was brutal. I can't bear to look at him so I leave the cubicle and head outside. I pass Adrian on the way out and tell him to come and get me when he knows what is happening with Sylvia.

  An hour passes until Adrian comes out to see me. It was an hour spent going over everything in my head. Why the fuck would he want to marry that woman? They have nothing in common and they don't even appear to like each other very much. She must make him feel young and vibrant in a way I never could...well if he thinks I'm getting arse implants he can fuck off. If I didn't know it before, I know now that my marriage is well and truly over and Archie has completely moved on. I need to concentrate on me and give thanks for everyone I have in my life. Thankfully Sylvia hasn't broken her hip, it's just badly bruised and she can go home. I ask Adrian to give her a hug from me and tell her I'll call her later. I don't want to tell her about Archie now...she'll be furious and I wouldn't put it past her to tip a bedpan over him.

I managed to get a few hours sleep when I got home. I actually slept quite well and I haven't got half the hangover I thought I was going to have. I had a chat with Jude about his Dad's impending marriage and he took it really well. He actually finds the prospect of Camilla becoming his Step-Mother quite amusing and of course it means he and Lola will be related. It's strange how life turns out isn't it...I think the universe is having a right old laugh at my expense. There's no point me going over and over Archie's decision because I'll never be able to fucking understand it. I just need to get on with my own life and make my own happiness. I finally get around to checking my phone and I've got dick, dick, dick and

Ralph. The dicks are hideous but Ralph looks fun. He's fifty five and a bus driver. He's not particularly good looking but he looks kind. He has a round jolly face and maybe he could be a laugh. Fuck it, I don't need handsome I just need faithful. I throw caution to the wind and message him back.

CHAPTER SIX

Ralph

Ralph and I have been chatting online and we are getting on like a house on fire. He's absolutely hilarious and I haven't laughed so much in ages. We're going for a walk in the park today...how very adult of us. He's bringing his dog and I'm really looking forward to some puppy time. I feel very positive about this one. I may not be off to the Caribbean to marry my lover but you can't beat an autumn stroll in the rain...who am I trying to kid? Archie has a wonderful new life and I'm a single, hormonal mess who can't remember what she went upstairs for and frequently calls her son by the hamster's name. I give myself a kick up the arse. I meant to enjoy today, not slip into a world of anxiety and regret. Bollocks to you,Archie...you may have Miss Perfection Personified but I may have my Ralphie by the end of the day. Feeling more optimistic, I dig out my waterproof coat and head to the park.

I'm outside the cafe waiting for him to arrive. My stomach is churning with a mixture of excitement, anticipation and anxiety and my head is full of 'what ifs'...what if he doesn't like me? What if I don't like him? What if he likes me and I like him? I take a deep breath and focus on what is going on around me. There's not too many people about, just hardened dog walkers and Sunday morning footballers...there's an awful lot of muscular thigh on display and it's improving the view no end.   Just as I'm thinking it might be a good idea to go and wait next to the football pitches I can see someone waving at me in the distance. I'm not sure if it's Ralph or not but wave back out of politeness. I don't think it is, as they appear to be leading a donkey...when you live in a seaside town it's not unusual to see donkeys in the most random of places.   As the figure gets closer it starts shouting 'Hey Ann'. It's definitely Ralph and it's not just his face that's round...he has a beer belly to behold and if we get to a point where we become intimate, I'm not sure I could find his cock beneath that thing. As for the donkey...it's his fucking dog. He said it was a puppy, he didn't say it was a St Bernard puppy...it's huge! Both Ralph and the monster dog bound over to me;

'Hi, Ann, good to finally meet you...meet Tiny.'

Before I can open my mouth 'Tiny' jumps up, places his massive paws on my shoulders and slobbers all over my face. Ralph lets out an enormous belly laugh as I wipe my face;

'He obviously likes you Ann...he's such a baby.'

He may be a baby and he is rather sweet but I've read Cujo by Stephen King and so I'll be keeping my distance just on the off chance he turns rabid. There's not an awful lot you can do when in possession of a monster dog other than walk and talk. Tiny is certainly popular as nearly everyone who passes us stops for a stroke and he's enjoying the attention so much he keeps slobbering over my shoes...remind me when I do eventually sack off men forever and fill my house full of dogs, to only opt for non slobbery breeds. I couldn't cope. Apart from Tiny's bad habits, I am enjoying Ralph's company. Do I fancy him? No, not really but I'm enjoying getting to know him and you never know he might just be able to laugh me into bed. Looks fade over time, a personality doesn't. We get a couple of takeaway coffees and sit under a sheltered bench to drink them. Tiny is worn out with all the attention and lies quietly by our feet. I think Ralph is also glad of the rest. I was getting a bit worried about him walking up hill...he looked red, sweaty and on the verge of a heart attack. He's making me howl with laughter with his bus driving anecdotes. He's endearing...like a human version of Tiny really;

'So Ann, what do you think, would you like to meet up again?'

Would I? Why the hell not...nothing ventured, nothing gained. Ralph is an absolute tonic. I haven't laughed so much in ages. We agree to meet tonight at a Mexican restaurant on the main road into town. Ralph kisses me on the cheek as he leaves and I wonder where all this is going to lead.

I haven't got long to get ready before I meet Ralph. Sylvia called me and kept me on the phone for ages. She was fuming about Archie and God help him the next time she sees him as she is definitely going to make her feelings known. Her hip is improving and she'll 'be back in action' in no time...Adrian will be pleased, although I do think he's probably been pleased to have a break. She's insatiable is our Sylvia. I have a quick bath, trim my muff just on the off chance I get the opportunity to try and find Ralph's cock...Jude is staying at a friends tonight so I have the house to myself. I straighten my hair and finally after dating in jeans for maybe too long, slip into a lovely, elegant black dress. I've kept my make-up fairly natural but have to wear my signature red lipstick...you are never too old for red lips. I have one last look in the mirror and you know what...I look good.

Ralph is waiting for me outside when I arrive at the restaurant. He looks really smart and has clearly made an effort, he greets me with one of his huge warm smiles and suddenly his spectacular paunch doesn't seem like a problem any more...I'm sure given the challenge I would be able to locate his cock. We take our seats at the table and whilst Ralph orders a pint of lager, I have a glass of coke. I'm giving alcohol a miss for a bit after my recent bad behaviour...I will also be keeping clear of any vegetables in the courgette, aubergine or marrow families. To play it safe I order the chicken chimichangas. Ralph has finished his pint before I finish looking at the menu and orders another...there's clearly no mystery as to where his beer belly comes from. Our food arrives and we have really started to bond, we actually have quite a lot in common. Ralph's wife left him for a much younger man (makes a fucking change) and he has a sixteen year old son who is currently dog sitting Tiny. When I tell him about Archie he understands completely where I'm coming from, we're like kindred spirits. He really is so funny, he's joking with the waiters and they love him. Ralph is great fun and I'm actually amazed he's still single. Just as we reach that point in the date where we start to make serious eye contact, I start to feel hot...really hot;

'Is it hot in here, Ralph...or is it just me?'

'I think it's just you Ann, we're sitting underneath the air conditioning so it's actually a little cool.'

Oh fuck, please not now...I'm not ready for a hot flush, it's most inconvenient. I try to ignore it the best I can but I feel my face start to burn;

'I'm so hot, Ralph.'

His response confuses me;

'You can say that again!'

He must have misunderstood me so I tell him again.

'I'm really, really hot, Ralph.'

I still don't think he gets it;

'Oh God yes, you are...you are so hot.'

I try one last time to get him to understand what I'm saying, maybe all those pints of lager have had an effect after all;

'I'm so hot, I think I'm going to have to get out of here.'

He really doesn't get it;

'I'm up for that. If I take a Viagra now, I'll be ready by the time we finish and get back to yours.'

If he takes a what now? For fuck's sake he thinks I'm hot, hot...he thinks I've got a fanny like Mount Vesuvius and I want to rip his clothes off and jump on board;

'No, no, sorry...I don't want to have sex with you. I'm hot because I'm going through the menopause and I'm having a hot flush.'

He looks momentarily confused and his response is like a red rag to a bull;

'Oh. I get it, your going through 'the change'.

I find myself remembering my conversation with Sylvia about 'the change' and deliver a rant to end all rants.

'The Change'...what the fuck is 'the change'? I hate that expression, it's like women hit a certain age, their periods stop overnight and they change into a fucking unicorn. It's not 'the change' it's the menopause and it doesn't happen in the blink of an eye. It takes a long time and it's not as easy 'the change' implies. I don't sleep well and if I do manage to sleep, I'm awake at five o'clock on the dot, my joints hurt...sometimes I feel like I've been kicked by a camel. My hair is untameable and frizzy...both on my head and on my chin. My memory is shot, I can't remember where I've put my phone when I'm speaking on it. I get anxious about the most stupid of things like putting my rubbish in the wrong recycling bin and when I do eventually get out of the house if I walk past a neighbour using a hose pipe, I have to run home to pee. My libido has fucked off and I wouldn't recognise a fanny tingle if it slapped me in the face. I get night sweats at night and hot flushes during the day...I feel like I'm a walking sauna. So no, I'm not going through 'the change' Ralph.'

A couple of women from the table next to us stand up and start clapping. Poor Ralph doesn't know where to look and I suddenly feel sorry for him. He thought he was getting a guaranteed shag and instead he had to listen to me ranting in a packed restaurant. I open my mouth to apologise but it's too late;

'I'm sorry Ann, I've got to dash. The dog is missing me.'

Oh the indignity, he's using my 'the dog is missing me' excuse to leave our date early. It's obviously true what they say about karma. He pays his half of the bill and gets out of the restaurant as quickly as he can. So I've been ditched twice in as many dates and I really can't be arsed thinking 'third time lucky'. I need to listen to the universe...dating is not for me. I need to take up a hobby...I believe knitting is quite popular, or bowls. I'm

Ann without an 'e', failed erotic or any other kind of Goddess, champion knitter and Crown Green Bowling champion. Feeling disillusioned yet again I head for the door. On my way out I'm stopped by the woman who was sitting on the table behind us;

'Sorry to bother you. I just wanted to say thank you for saying what you did. My husband has never been able to get his head around the menopause. He thought I was just a moody cow who didn't want to have sex. Listening to you this evening has really opened his eyes and you might just have saved my marriage.'

I'm fucking delighted. If I've helped just one woman by sharing my thoughts, then tonight wasn't a total disaster. That lovely lady has just turned my evening around and I feel quite pleased with myself. I'm adamant that I'm not dating again but maybe I'm not ready for bowls just yet.

I get home and check my phone. To my surprise there's not a cock to be seen and I have two messages from two rather gorgeous looking men. I'm tempted for a split second but really can"t be arsed so delete them and then delete the dating app. What the fuck was I thinking? I'm a walking disaster when it comes to men and I'm not going to go looking for romance ever again...if it just happens to drop into my lap then so be it but I'm not putting myself through this again. I'm just about to take myself off to bed when my phone rings...it's Ryan;

'They're getting married Ann. Archie and Camilla they're going to get married in the Caribbean. So that's it, it really is over.'

He sounds so upset. I don't really know what to say...there's nothing to say really,is there? I arrange to pop over to his tomorrow for a coffee. It will be easier to talk to him face to face. Hopefully by tomorrow he will have come to terms with it a bit more....the last thing I need is more drama.

CHAPTER SEVEN

Ryan

I had another restless nights sleep, so much to think about and not a lot I can do about it. I understand why Ryan is upset. Finding out that Archie and Camilla are getting married is the final nail in the coffin, confirmation that that's that. It's also a tad insulting that they can move on so quickly, like all those years of marriage never actually happened. Well fuck them...I've had enough of being the victim and I'm going to get on with my life and be happy despite them. I'm also totally confident in my decision to give the whole dating thing a miss. If I'm meant to meet someone else then I'll meet them. I'm leaving my relationship status in the hands of fate and feel much better for it. I'm worthy of so much more than the way Archie treated me, why should I settle for second or third best? I've decided, I'll let him have his divorce as quickly as possible. What's the point in delaying the inevitable apart from the satisfaction of denying Miss Fucking Perfection Personified her Caribbean wedding. The sooner I can detach myself from the whole shit show the better.

Once Jude as gone to school, I head to Ryan's. I really don't know what to expect. He sounded so upset last night. I'm pleasantly surprised when he answers the door, he seems remarkably upbeat. I haven't been into his house since before the Archie and Camilla debacle and it has completely changed. When Camilla move in she stripped the house of it's Bohemian, arty character. It became white and clinical and all traces of Ryan's artistry where removed. I'm so pleased to see he's restored it to it's original style, it's just how I remember it all those years ago;

'I love what you've done with the house, Ryan. I feel like I've gone back in time.'

'I never liked the clinical look, it just wasn't me. I went along with it to humour Camilla.'

He went along with a lot to humour that woman and it till got him nowhere. He makes me a cup of coffee and we sit in the living room. The colourful throws and comfy cushions are back and the walls are adorned with Ryan's artwork. How could she be so cruel as to make him take down all his fabulous drawings and paintings, they are part of who he is.

'What is it about her Ryan? I've only ever loved two men in my life and she took them both.'

I inwardly cringe, why did I say that? He knew I loved him though, he said he loved me...but why did I have to bring it up, I'm such a twat;

'I can't explain it Ann. She's magnetic...she draws you in and then when you reach the point of no return she grinds you down so you don't have the energy to move on. When she sees something that she wants, she goes all out to get it. I did love you, Ann, but she got into my head...put distance between us and once she'd reeled me in there was no going back. After I spoke to you last night, I realised that actually Archie has done me a favour. We've pretty much lived separate lives since Lola was born and I didn't see it until now. She wasn't interested in me or her daughter. She enjoyed the attention she got at my art exhibitions or a gallery opening but not the family stuff. Can you imagine Camilla at a theme park or paddling in the sea? Camilla loves Camilla and nobody else will come close. Archie is in the honeymoon period at the moment and once she's got that ring on her finger it will be over before their real honeymoon has begun. Over the years I've often wondered what would have happened if I'd never met her, would we have got married?..I treated you badly Ann and I'm so very sorry.'

Well that's a revelation. There's no point looking back though. If Ryan hadn't dumped me for Camilla, I wouldn't have got together with Archie and we wouldn't have Jude and Lola who are the best things to come out of our relationships;

'I do forgive you, Ryan. We both just need to look to the future now, we did have some fun though didn't we? Whatever happened to the portrait you did of me?'

'Camilla wanted me to destroy it but I just couldn't so I hid it in the loft. Give me a couple of minutes and I'll go and find it.'

Typical she wanted my picture ceremoniously burnt, probably as some sort of gift to whichever evil God she worships. As Ryan goes off to find my portrait, I feel more relaxed than I have in a long time. Finally I think we both have everything straight in our heads and rather than an ending, we see a bright new beginning;

'Here you go, Ann...weren't you beautiful!'

What does he mean 'wasn't I'...cheeky twat. The picture is fabulous, I'm slimmer and look, there's no lines on my face and I have a fabulous firm jaw line. I suddenly feel all nostalgic for my dating days...the mangled manhood, roller skating catastrophe and dogging disaster bring a smile to my face...the good old days! Suddenly a thought pops into my head which typically I vocalise before thinking it through...I don't think I will ever learn;

'Can we do another one? Another portrait Ryan...then we'd have a before and after.'

There's a moment of silence before he answers and I wonder if I've offended him in some way?

'Ann, that is a brilliant idea. You know the routine, there's a dressing gown on the back of the bedroom door. Go and get ready and I'll get my stuff together.'

I go into Ryan's bedroom and get undressed. What the fuck am I doing?...I'm fifty years old I should be baking banana bread not posing naked for my ex-boyfriend. I wrap myself in Ryan's dressing gown and when I get downstairs he's waiting for me, pencil in hand. I take off my dressing gown and Ryan doesn't flinch...he's in serious artist mode and nothing will deflect him from the job in hand. Feeling ever so self-conscious, I drape myself on the sofa. My once pert breasts have gone south and the only way for me to stop my thighs rubbing together would be to adopt a gynaecological pose and that would be a whole new level of portrait painting. Once again I feel like the woman in Titanic, only this time it's her elderly version but all power to me...I'm channelling my inner erotic Goddess again and I like it. Ryan begins to draw and after about ten minutes he stops;

'You are still beautiful, Ann...in fact you are more beautiful than ever.'

Did he really just say that...Is he deluded or does he need glasses?

'Really. You've matured like a fine wine.'

A can of Stella more like.

'Your body is amazing. Think what it did, it nurtured and grew Jude. Every stretch mark is a testament to what it achieved.'

So, he may have a point but did he really need to mention my stretch marks? Thankfully he stops talking and gets on with drawing. After another half an hour my left leg is starting to feel numb;

'Are you nearly done, Ryan?'

'Just about finished.'

My relief at him nearly finishing is suddenly replace by utter horror as the door to the living room opens and Jude and Lola fly in. Jude screams, Lola laughs and Ryan is so engrossed in his drawing he doesn't notice;

'MUM?' shouts Jude.

'DAD?' howls Lola.

Fuck, fuck ,fuck. I grab the dressing gown off the floor to cover myself up. Thankfully the settee has a high back so I don't think they saw anything...please God don't let them have seen anything. Ryan finally registers that our children are in the room and he looks like a rabbit caught in the headlights;

'Jude, Lola...it's not what it looks like. Ann wanted me to draw her naked.'

Marvellous Ryan, put all the blame on me. I've probably just traumatised my child for life;

'Jude, I'm so sorry. It really is innocent...what are you doing out of school?'

'The heating went off so they sent us home. You should have had a text but clearly you don't have your phone on you. Me and Lola were saying you and her Dad should get together and I'm happy for you, just try and keep it a bit more private. We're going to go and get a milkshake so I'll see you later.'

With that, as quickly as they entered the room, they left. I feel well and truly told off and what was all that me and

Ryan nonsense? How could they possibly think me and him would be good idea after everything that has gone on? I run upstairs to get dressed and when I get back down Ryan is waiting with the portrait;

'So what do you think, will it do?'

Will it do? It will more than do it was amazing.

'Ryan, I love it. Thank you so much.'

'There's nothing to thank me for, Ann...it's all you and as I said before you are beautiful. Can you believe they came back! I'm going to get a right bollocking from Lola when she gets home. You know what they said about me and you getting together...how do you fancy going on a date? Lets put the past behind us and give it a go. You've made me see that there's life beyond Camilla.'

I can't quite believe that he thinks we would be a good idea but going on one date wouldn't do any harm, would it? At least there wouldn't be any nasty surprises;

'I'm not sure Ryan. You broke my heart all those years ago when you left me for Miss Fucking Perfection Personified. At the time I thought you were the 'one' I thought we had a future together. We've overcome all the bad feeling between us and we've become friends...our children are friends. I'm not sure it's worth risking those friendships.'

He looks confused and a little hurt;

'Who is Miss Fucking Perfection Personified...is it Camilla?'

Of course it's fucking Camilla...for goodness sake.

'That's my nickname for her. She's perfect, everything any man could ever want.'

'She's far from perfect! Cunning, manipulative, cold and uncaring, definitely. Perfect, absolutely not. I treated you badly and I can't tell you how much I regret it. I made the

Mother of all mistakes all those years ago and I have truly paid for it. I'm not asking you to marry me Ann. I'm just asking you to come round and let me cook you a meal, how does spaghetti carbonara followed by chocolate profiteroles sound?'

He remembered they were my favourites, he's grooming me with food. I'm still not sure...he was pining for Camilla last night and now he's had an awakening and he's glad to be rid? Oh fuck it, it's not like I've got much else going on at the moment is it?

'Fine, let's give a date a go but remember, I'm not your rebound option and I'm not shagging you...you've got a lot to prove before you get anywhere near my fanny.'

'That's what I loved about you, Ann, your fantastic way with words. Why beat around the bush when you can just come straight out and say it. How does tomorrow night suit you. I'll send Lola over to yours and give them some money for a takeaway. It won't be a late night, I'll have you home by ten. However, there is one rule...we don't talk about them.'

Well, events have taken a surprising turn from yesterday. I'm going on a date with Ryan...it's not really a date though is it, more like old friends having a good old catch up and it's a school day tomorrow so as Ryan said I'll be home by ten. Whatever happens, I'm taking this slowly. Maybe me and Ryan will work, maybe we won't. The most important thing is that whatever happens we retain our friendship. The world is full of cocks but a good friend is hard to find. We say our goodbyes and I wonder what tomorrow will bring.

CHAPTER EIGHT

Ryan yet again

I haven't stopped today...it's hard work trying to make yourself look presentable.

After a long conversation with Sylvia where she told me to get a grip and fucking go for it, I've had my hair cut, I really needed to sort out the frizz. I wasn't sure the hairdresser knew what the hell I was talking about when I asked her to sort out my menopausal minge head but she's done a great job...I have soft bouncy curls and if I can avoid any moisture, they might even last until tonight. I've had my eyebrows threaded and after years of politely declining, finally relented and let her do my chin. Using pliers is ridiculous and just one step away from getting the gardeners in ...however at the rate it's growing that day will probably soon come. I bought myself a new dress and I may just have purchased some new lingerie...big pants as always and the most fabulous push up bra. I went for red, well it's a classic isn't it? Not that I'm going to be showing them off at all...sex is off the menu. I bought them to give me confidence, so I feel sexy. It doesn't matter that I'm fifty, it doesn't matter that I'm menopausal, I can still look attractive and desirable...age is just a fucking number and we really do worry about it far to much. The past few months have really dented my confidence, the menopause has dented my confidence and I need to start working on getting it back. I'm determined to grab the menopause by the horns and kick it up the arse, it's taken far too much from my life and I'm not going to let it take another thing.

Once I get home from town, I have a long soak in the bath. I try a tightening face mask in an attempt to give gravity a kick up the arse and give my muff a 'just in case' but 'most likely not' trim. I can't help wondering if Ryan's performance has improved over the years. When I was with him he was a two minute wonder who got what he wanted out of sex, rolled over and went to sleep...something tells me Camilla would have let him get away with that. I suppose I'll just have to wait and see and depending on how things pan out, I might never get my answer. Once out of the bath, I slather on some body cream that's been in my drawer since last Christmas...not sure it smells quite right but it's too late now I'm covered in it. I put on my chest high knickers and posh bra and look in the mirror...I'm happy with that. I can even live with my arse cheeks trying to escape the fabric because I am what I am and I will not conform to pressure to become stick thin. I have tits (finally) and an arse...and I fucking love them. Once I've put my dress on, I do my make-up and I'm ready to go. Ryan is dropping off Lola here and I'm going back to his house with him. As I walk down the stairs Jude appears from the kitchen;

'Wow Mum, you look lovely.'

Well that was a compliment indeed. Usually all I get from Jude is 'you're not wearing that are you?' Apparently I embarrass him at school when I wear my Dr. Martens...they are far too young for me. I also embarrass him when I open my mouth, breath or even attempt to speak to his friends. However, the fire escape incident has given me some kudos...I might not be allowed back into the school again but the kids think I'm great. There's a knock on the door which signals Ryan's arrival. My tummy is in knots...why am I so nervous it's not as if we don't know each other? I open the door to the lovely Lola and the first thing she does is compliment me on my appearance. I beginning to think there is something funny going on here. Lola moves out of the way and Ryan stands in my doorway slightly open mouthed;

'You look absolutely stunning!'

Okay, what's the score...do I usually look like shit and the fact that I've made an effort has completely shocked everyone? I decide not to think about it too deeply and just take the compliment...heaven knows when you get to my age you don't get that many. I shout goodbye to Jude who is now on the games console with Lola...they grunt a goodbye which is fairly standard. I don't quite know what to say on the short journey to Ryan's house so talk about the weather and the new school timetable. This has all happened so quickly...who would have thought...me and Ryan going on a date?

When we arrive at Ryan's we head straight for the living room. He's really made an effort, the table is set beautifully and the room is full of candles...he's going to be in for a disappointment if this is a full on seduction routine. Ryan brings me a glass of Prosecco and I make a mental note not to have more than two glasses...I need to keep a clear head to make sure I don't try and give him a sympathy wank like I did with Frank. The food smells divine...he always did make a fantastic spaghetti carbonara. We talk about anything and everything as we eat and, as agreed, the only subject that's off limits is Archie and Camilla. Tonight is about us not them. True to his word, once we finish our main course Ryan brings me the most amazing bowl of chocolate profiteroles...if he's trying to get to my fanny through my stomach he's onto a winner with these, they are delicious. As I'm eating I look at him across the table. He's still everything I remember him to be...muscular, with that impressively square jaw. His hair is greying and his face is lined (who wouldn't have lines after living with Camilla for all those years) but he is still fabulously handsome. I think I might feel a bit of desire creeping in. It's not the alcohol as I've only had one glass...now this is all getting a bit confusing. I didn't want to fancy him but I do, I really do. I can't come across as too keen, we are friends and I'm not going to jump headlong or fannylong into anything.

After we finish out profiteroles, I take the plates into the kitchen and offer to wash up...that's what friends do isn't it? Ryan is the perfect gentleman and tells me he won't hear of it...I'm a guest in his house and he wants me to relax and enjoy myself...oh God how I want to relax and enjoy myself. I make myself comfortable on the settee whilst Ryan sorts out the kitchen...he's incredibly well house trained, had to be, I guess, because somehow I can't imagine Camilla sticking her hands in the sink to do the washing up. I can't imagine Camilla doing anything other than concentrate on her appearance. Archie is going to find that really difficult, he works such long hours the last thing he is going to want to do when he gets home is tidy up after Miss Fucking Perfection Personified. Well tough shit Archie...you made your bed and you can lie in it. Ryan sits by me on the settee, refills my glass and puts his arm around my shoulders. I feel myself snuggling into his chest;

'I've had such a lovely evening Ann, you are a real star...you make my soul sing.'

Shit, he's gone all arty and ethereal on me...I make his soul sing, what does that mean exactly? It sounds like it's a good thing;

'Thanks...but I don't have a clue what that means.'

'It means I've finally seen the light and I've finally realised that you make me happy, Ann.'

With that, he gently lifts my face and leans in for a kiss. Suddenly all my doubts fly out of the window and I'm more than happy to oblige. It's a deep, probing kiss full of passion and desire. He reaches into my bra and removes my breast gently sucking on my nipple as his hand starts to move up my leg, I'm feeling breathless. His hand moves higher and higher and before I know it he's gently stroking me, I can feel he's about to move inside my pants. My fanny isn't tingling but I can feel something stirring in my brain. I have a longing, a desire and yet again I articulate it without thinking;

'Ryan, I'd love a nice cup of tea and a slice of cake if you have any.'

For fuck's sake...fuck you menopause brain. The nearest thing I've got to a shag in months and all I fancy is a cup of tea.

'I'm so sorry Ryan. I really thought I did want to but my hormones are pretty fucked and my libido has done one. It's gone, left the building, fucked right off.'

I go on to explain how the menopause has been affecting me over the past few months. I tell him everything and he listens patiently without judgement. I even tell him about my rant in the restaurant when I was out with Ralph, he finds it hilarious and hopes somebody filmed it and puts it on TikTok so he can see me in all my menopausal glory. I, on the other hand really hope nobody did film it...I'm not ready to go viral just yet. He is so sympathetic and lovely. I find his attitude really refreshing and feel like he really understands;

'I'm here for you, Ann, and I'll help you through it every step of the way. I really do want us to be more than friends and I'm happy to wait as long as it takes...what do you think, are you up for dating an ageing artist?'

This all feels so right...Ryan still has a way to go to prove he won't let me down again but he's doing bloody brilliantly so far. Maybe just maybe this could work;

'I'd love to!'

He kisses me again and for the first time in what feels like forever I'm happy. Ryan brings me my cup of tea and even manages to rustle up a slice of chocolate cake. The tea is just what I needed and the cake is divine...I'm clearly easily pleased. As I get ready to leave, Ryan hands me a large parcel. I open it and it's both the portraits he did of me...framed and ready to go on the wall;

'Ryan, I don't know what to say...thank you so much.'

'You don't need to say anything, just look at them to remind yourself how beautiful you are.'

I feel myself starting to blush. Though where on earth I could hang them up in my house I don't know...Jude is not going to want to look at pictures of his Mother naked no matter how artistic they are. Imagine what his friends would say, it doesn't bear thinking about! He would never be able to live it down...his Mum on the wall with her tits out. Maybe I'll put them right at the back of the wardrobe and look at them from time to time. They can go on the wall when Jude leaves home.

Ryan drives me home and I feel confident about the future. He kisses me tenderly as I get out of the car and we agree to meet up again as soon as possible. No sooner do I get through the front door and my phone pings with a text from Ryan;

'Looking forward to the future, Ann.'

They say never look back but maybe looking back could be the best thing that ever happened to me. Fate works in strange ways. Obviously, Ryan and I weren't meant to be at the time but we remained linked by our children. It could be that now is our time...who knows?

CHAPTER NINE

Lessons learnt

Ryan and I have been dating for the last three months and so far, so fucking fantastic. We are both officially divorced and Archie and Miss Fucking Perfection Personified have had their Caribbean wedding...I hope it rained! Jude has finally agreed to visit his Dad if Camilla is there as long as he goes with Lola and, according to them, once the ring was on Camilla's finger she started making Archie's life hell. It's all panning out just as Ryan predicted and I can't say I have any sympathy for

Archie whatsoever. He wanted Camilla and now he's got her in all her evil glory. I took Sylvia's advice and went to see the doctor about my menopause. I've been put on HRT and I'm feeling more like me than I have in a long time. You have options and if your GP isn't sympathetic, find another one...you don't need to suffer the menopause, there is so much help available and I've learnt a lot by just going online. I know some women can't, or don't want to, go on HRT but there are other things you can do to improve your symptoms. Talk to women going through similar, join groups on Facebook...you are not alone. As for my sex life...I am Ann without the 'e', erotic Goddess and shagger extraordinaire. Ryan has more than improved his performance over the years and he's certainly taught me a thing or two. I'm sleeping much better and my sleep is only disturbed by Ryan who just can't get enough of me when we are together. I've been given a new lease of life and it's fantastic. I thought my life had ground to a halt when Archie left me...I couldn't have been more wrong. It was a wonderful new beginning and I've learnt to grab every opportunity with both hands.

So apart from the reverse cowgirl, what else have I learnt? Even the most reliable of people can let you down, I thought me and Archie would be together forever and look how that turned out. He thought he deserved better than me and that better was Miss Fucking Perfection Personified. I'll never know what he saw in her, maybe she made him feel young, maybe she was a great shag, maybe he was really into huge tits? What I do know, is that I'm blissfully happy and she's making his life a fucking misery. The grass really isn't always greener on the other side, Archie. My marriage ended and at the time, I never thought I would get over the hurt but it's amazing how things turn around...there's always sunshine after the rain and I found mine in Ryan.

When men hit their fifties and start wearing ripped jeans, tight tops and Cuban heels they have possibly hit a mid-life crisis. If they also start driving a very expensive open topped sports car then they are definitely trying to recapture their youth. If they start referring to themselves by a cringe worthy nickname such as 'Big D' then leg it, run for the hills as they clearly have ambitions to appear on some sort of reality TV show where they'll be surrounded by young women swooning over their wealth and experience. If they want to make complete dicks of themselves by chasing their youth then leave them to it. They are obviously insecure in their own skin and you really don't need that shit. Be confident in yourself and live your best life. Age has nothing on experience...never forget it. Daniel has always been my favourite fantasy but the sight of him dripping in ice cold water chasing after a woman young enough to be his daughter killed it forever. As for Doug and his essay of unreasonable demands...fuck that for a game of soldiers. You never have to comply with a man's demands. If they want you to fit in their box then tell them to shove that box up their arse. You are your own person and you don't have to change to suit anyone. Some of the best women I know swear, burp and fart with pride. It's also important to learn that when you need to make a quick exit, check that you are not going to set a fire alarm off and disrupt a whole school day. I'm may have been elevated to 'cool Mum' status but the headteacher hates me.

Men never grow out of sending dick pics. I think it's wired into their brains...'If she sees my dick then I'm going to get a guaranteed shag.' Well sorry chaps you are so, so wrong. I want to get to know you from the waist up first. You could have the world's greatest cock but if you are a twat I'm don't want to know. Which brings me onto the lovely Frank. He was such a nice man but still madly in love with his wife. You must never settle for being second best...it will never work. Not that I got the opportunity to even try and compete. Which brings me onto another important lesson I learnt...at the age of fucking fifty. Don't get carried away on the Prosecco. Know your limitations or you'll end up comparing vegetables to cocks and offending a lovely man who thinks you are laughing at his cock. Poor Frank, I wonder if he did eventually find his wife substitute?

We all need to be more like Sylvia. She lives her best life and doesn't let her age dictate her life in any way at all. She lets nothing hold her back and lives every day to the full, she doesn't conform to any of the stereotypes of age. Who would have thought that a woman in her seventies could have so much fun on a sex swing. I'll be honest with you, until she mentioned it, I didn't even know what a sex swing was. She gave us all such a scare when she fell and when she got home, I did suggest she maybe packed the swing away but she was having none of it;

'The day I stop wearing my flamingo mask in public and put my sex swing away is the day I die.'

This was a bit of a revelation for both me and Adrian...where the fuck was she wearing her mask in public? I thought her dogging days ended when she met him...don't tell me she's the grande dame of the local dogging circuit? Well that's a discussion for Adrian to have with her, I'm keeping well out of it. Sylvia is the epitome of growing old disgracefully and I want to be just like her. She's so happy about me and Ryan but she did welcome him into our little family with stern warning;

'You ever hurt her again and I'll be wearing your balls for earrings.'

So that was Ryan told...you really don't want to get on the wrong side of Sylvia.

Don't be afraid to talk about the menopause, rant and rave as much as you want to get your point across. Your symptoms are real and don't let anyone minimise what you are going through because they don't understand. When I was having a hot flush, Ralph thought I was hot because I was desperate to jump into bed with him...he was even ready to take a Viagra so he was shag ready. My rant in the restaurant set him straight...the fucking 'change'...if only it was that simple. I didn't care that Ralph looked like a classic 1970's comedian, he was funny and warm and until the moment he thought I was gagging for him he could have been a prospect. He made the assumption that I wanted to sleep with him and that let him down. I really do believe that looks don't matter if someone has a good heart and a corking personality, he really did make me laugh. I could even have learnt to live with Tiny the slobbering puppy from the depths of hell.

You can find happiness in the most unexpected places. Who would have thought I would have ended up back in Ryan's arms? I love having a sneaky peak at the pictures he did of me...they make me feel empowered. I'm Ann without the 'e', erotic Goddess, nude model and now stupidly happy. Obviously it's still in the back of my mind that he cheated on me once and he could do it again but I also have to remember that it was many years ago and people do mature and change. I couldn't be that unlucky that another Miss Fucking Perfection Personified would appear on the scene...could I?Jude and Lola are absolutely delighted, they have been like brother and sister for so many years and now they feel like it's official. They broke the news to Archie and Camilla that we were together and she was absolutely fuming, she clearly didn't want either of us to be happy...well bollocks to you Camilla we are happier than you will ever know. Archie didn't express and opinion either way and you know what, I really don't care. He's not the man I thought he was, he's moved on and so have I. There's no point going over and over what happened. I'm happy now and I do truly hope that he does find happiness with Camilla, though it does make me feel a little smug to think that actually, she's going to give him a really hard time...tough shit Archiewoowoo. So that's me married, divorced and now happily dating Ryan (again). I've said it before and I'll say it again, be happy and never let anyone piss on your bonfire. There's only one you and you are fucking fantastic. Keep you fingers crossed for me and Ryan but I think, finally, I've found my Mr Romance and my Mr Uninhibited.

If you haven't read the first book in the 'Wax and Whips' series ('Wax Whips and my Hairy Bits') here's the first few pages...

Wax Whips and My Hairy Bits...

CHAPTER ONE

Me

I used to love reading romance novels, nothing modern, just good old fashioned Victorian romantic literature. It was a time of innocence, the pace of life was slower, the men more charming. A time where you didn't have to conform to female stereotypes online, where you never needed to ask 'does my arse look big in this' because everyone looked big in a bustle and no fucker was going to get a look at your arse until you had a ring on your finger. It gave me hope that there was a Mr Romance out there for us all and then suddenly it dawned on me that actually it was all a little bit dull. It took me a bit of time to realise where it was all going wrong, but then it became clear. These novels, lovely as they were, were missing one vital component...they didn't do cock.

My name is Ann, not regal Anne, just plain, boring, unexciting Ann. I often wonder how my life would have turned out if my parents had just given me that extra 'e'. I am thirty-two years old, no spring chicken and no stranger to the dating scene. I work in marketing which isn't as glamorous as it sounds and if I'm honest it bores the shit out of me. The search for my Mr Romance had led me to a succession of short, infuriating relationships where the sex had been no more exciting than a blow job and a quick shag (missionary position). I needed less Mr Romance and more Mr Uninhibited. I needed excitement, hot wax and a fucking good seeing to. I was single, more than ready to mingle and had read a shit load of Erotica so I knew exactly what I had to do in order to embark on a new sexual adventure. I wanted no strings sex, none of that emotional bollocks, just a good hard fuck and maybe a cup of coffee in the morning. I'm bored of feeling boring. I don't want to be Ann who's a good laugh, I want to be Ann who's amazing in bed, I want to be the shag that stays with you a lifetime, never bettered or forgotten.

My longest relationship had lasted nearly two years, Hayden. We met when we were both at university. I was so young and inexperienced I didn't really know what a good shag was. I lost my virginity to him after four bottles of Diamond White and maybe it was because I was pissed, or maybe because he was shit at shagging, but it was a completely underwhelming experience. There was no earth shaking orgasm, just the feeling something was missing and a sore fanny for a couple of days. We muddled along, foreplay was always the same, I gave him a blow job, he tried to find my clitoris…the man needed a fucking map. Sex was nearly always missionary, I'd sneak on top whenever I could, but he'd always flip me over for a quick finish. Maybe we just became too familiar with each other but when he started to not take his socks off when we had a shag I knew it was time to move on. He wasn't that arsed to be honest, I think he'd started to prefer his games console to me anyway and if he could have stuck his knob in it I'm sure he would have dumped me before I dumped him. My relationship history since Hayden has been unremarkable, hence my decision to ditch the romance novels and dive head long, or should that be muff long, into Erotica.

I'm suppose you could say I'm reasonably pretty and my face is holding up well, which is surprising given my twenty a day smoking habit, absolute love of kebabs and a probable dependency on Prosecco. My tits aren't too bad, they measure in at a 36C and I'm pleased to say they are still nice and perky and probably a few years off resembling a Spaniel's ears. My legs are long and shapely and the cellulite on my arse can be hidden with a good, supportive pair of knickers. Thongs just aren't going to happen, sorry Erotica but negotiating with a piece of cheese wire up my arse does not do it for me whatsoever. I've been researching my subject well recently, and one of the first rules when embarking on an erotic adventure seems to be that one must have a shaven haven, a freshly mown lawn, a smooth muff…I think you get the picture. I need to think carefully about how I am going to achieve my erotica ready fanny as the expression 'bearded clam' doesn't describe the half of it!

I don't fancy having my fanny flaps waxed and shaving isn't really an option as I'm petrified I'll get a shaving rash. So the only option I've got is hair remover cream. A quick trip to the shops and it's mission accomplished; my lady garden is smothered in intimate hair remover cream. It looks like a Mr Whippy with sprinkles but definitely no chocolate flake. It's not the most attractive look in the world, I'm staggering around like a saddle sore old cowboy, but it's going to be worth it…I am Ann without an 'e' and without pubes, a bald fannied paragon of sexual liberation. That bird with the posh name in 50 shades of whatever is going to have nothing on me! Though I have to admit, the undercarriage was a bit of a nightmare and to be honest it does sting a bit. At least I don't have to wait too long and then I will be smooth, shiny and....ouch...I'm fucking burning now! Burning is not right surely? Jesus, my flaps are on fire. Give me a minute I need to jump in the shower and get this shit off.

I just spent four fucking hours in A&E. I washed the cream off and my minge was glowing red and burning like a bastard which was almost bearable until the swelling started. I could feel my lips starting to throb, they were pulsating like a rare steak. I didn't want to look down, but I knew I had to…fuck me I had testicles, just call me Johnny Big Bollocks because that is what I had. I quickly checked Dr Google and the best thing for swelling is elevation and an ice pack, so I spent the best part of half an hour with my minge in the air and a packet of frozen peas clamped between my thighs. Needless to say it had no effect at all and it became painfully clear that I was going to have to haul my now damp, swollen crotch to the hospital. Never before have I felt so humiliated, having to describe in intimate detail my problem to little Miss Smug Bitch at reception;

'So, you've come to A&E today because your vagina is swollen'...

...well it's my vulva actually but let's not split pubic hairs, or try and get them off with cunting hair remover cream.   Sour face huffed and puffed and eventually booked me in, I spent what felt like an eternity pacing around...I couldn't sit down, my testicles wouldn't allow it and by this time a ball bra wouldn't have gone amiss. The Doctor I saw, who was absolutely gorgeous (the one time I didn't want to show an attractive man my fanny) and, when he wasn't stifling a laugh, couldn't have been more sympathetic. I'd had an allergic reaction and he'd prescribe me some anti-histamines which would bring the swelling down, my labia would return to their normal size and other than some skin sensitivity for a few days I would be fine but under no circumstances was I to use hair remover cream again as next time the reaction could be even worse.   Though what could be worse than the whopping set of bollocks I'd grown I don't know.   So that's that, I'm going to have to go au natural. Which is fine by me, I'd rather have a hairy beaver than an angry one.

A few hours later and my muff has more or less returned to normal and other than feeling slightly itchy seems to be perfectly fine. I've crossed shaven haven off my to do list and need to carry on with my preparation. As you may have already gathered, I've got a lot of work to do. I've noticed in most of the Erotica I've read that the words penis and vagina are rarely used, so I need to practise my sexual vocabulary, I need to learn how to talk dirty...I need to do my Erotica homework. I've had another flick through some of my books and there's no way I can call my vagina 'my sex' I know strictly speaking it is, but for fuck's sake...'my sex craves you', 'my sex needs your sex' it's all sounds a bit contrived if you ask me so I think I'll check out the Urban Dictionary.

I've just spent a good hour trawling through and my God what an education that was. Either I'm more wet behind the ears than I thought I was or some of the things I've just read are made up, check out 'Angry Pirate'...that's not for real, is it? I'm ready to try some of the new words and phrases I've learnt. I need to be all pouty lipped and doe eyed as I look in the mirror, moisten my lips and purr:

'I want to suck your length'

'Do you want to drink out of my cream bucket'

'My clit is hard and ready to be licked'

'My vagina is the most magical place in the world, come inside'

What the fuck was I thinking, I can't say this shit! Firstly the doe eyed, pouty lip thing makes me look like I'm pissed and secondly I can't do this without laughing. I'm much more comfortable with 'do you fancy a pint of Guinness and a quick shag'. I quickly give my head a wobble, comfortable is boring. I'm in this for the excitement and the clit tingling thrill (see I did learn something). Maybe I'll just opt for quiet and mysterious, let my body do the talking and my mouth do the sucking (I'm really starting to get this now). So that's the plan, my persona will be a sultry erotic goddess who doesn't say much, I'll be irresistible, a fabulous shag who doesn't want a conversation, no chat just sex.

The last part of my preparation is what on earth am I going to wear? If I'm going for the mysterious look does that mean I'm going to have to channel my inner sex goddess, or does it mean I go for a prim and proper, hair up, professional look? Maybe a combination of both, tight fitting dress, hair up and glasses, then I can do the whole taking my glasses off and flicking my hair down thing. The hair flicking thing however is a bit of an issue for me: my hair is naturally curly...really curly, at university my nickname was 'pube head' which probably tells you all you need to know, so I'm going to have to straighten it to within an inch of its life. From frump to fox...check me out. Today is going to be an exciting day. I'm just waiting for the postman to arrive, I've ordered some proper lingerie. I've gone for two sets initially, traditional black and racy red. Shit, should I have ordered a dildo? I forgot about a fucking dildo and candles, I forgot candles! What about a butt plug...what actually is a butt plug? I can't be erotic if I'm not dripping hot wax on him whilst pleasuring myself with a multi speed vibrating dildo...okay, so maybe not at the same time but you get my drift. Handcuffs! Shit, I'm not very good at this, he'll just have to tie me up with my big knickers.

The postman came, and I swear he had a knowing glint in his eye when he asked me to sign for my delivery or maybe he just read the label on the back of the parcel, cheeky bastard.   It took me a while to build up the courage but here I am, standing in front of a full length mirror wearing a bright red, lacy push up bra, matching arse covering comfortable pants, a suspender belt and black stockings. I'm not sure. My tits are standing to attention and look like boiled eggs in a frilly egg cup, they are virtually dangling from my ear lobes and I swear you can see my minge stubble.   So the new plan will be to go for subdued or even better, no lighting at all. I think it's all starting to look really erotic… bushy fanny, no filthy talking and everything done in the dark. The scene is set and I'm ready to get out there. No strings, erotic sex here I come. Well, not quite, I need to sign up to a dating site.

I take a selfie of myself looking as sultry as possible (not doe eyed or pouty, we know that doesn't work) I decide to show a little bit of cleavage and a little bit of leg, but not too much I want to leave my potential dates gagging to see more…I'm such a temptress. I've written and rewritten my profile about twenty times, it has to be just right and I think on my twenty first attempt I've finally done it:

'Flirty thirty two year old,

I work in marketing,

I like to get my head down in both the boardroom and the bedroom,

I'm looking for no strings attached fun,

Hobbies include reading, cooking and amateur dramatics.'

I know, you don't have to tell me, it's painfully shit. Hopefully they'll just look at my profile picture and to be honest at this point I don't care, I've submitted everything and I am now a fully paid up member of a dating site.

It takes a couple of hours for my phone to eventually ping with a notification that I have a message, I'm trembling with excitement as I open it...

'You've got nice tits'

Fuck me, 'You've got nice tits' is that it? I mean it's nice he thinks I've got nice tits, but I was expecting a little bit more. No, hang on he's sent a picture...it's a dick! He's sent me a picture of his dick, eww I don't think I've ever seen such a stumpy little penis, it's got a hugely bulbous bellend which looks like it's going to explode at any minute and hang on, it looks like it's winking at me…I'm never going to be able to unsee that! I quickly delete the message, when my phone pings again…It's another dick, not the same dick, this one is long, thin and veiny as fuck. Maybe I'm being too fussy, knobs aren't supposed to be attractive are they? My phone is quickly becoming a rogues gallery of ugly shlongs. I'm really starting to think maybe this wasn't a good idea, I know I said I wanted plenty of cock, but this wasn't exactly what I meant. Three cocks later and just as I am about to give up on the whole idea (maybe a pint of Guinness and a quick shag isn't too bad after all) I get a message from Daniel. I check out his profile and he actually looks quite fit, he's good looking, athletic and he didn't send me a dick pic....

What happens next?...buy the book to find out!

And...while I have you here I'd like to recommend another book of mine. The book is called 'Fakes, Freaks, Liars and Cheats' and it's an outrageous thriller set in the world of celebrity that is by turns very funny, shockingly outrageous and very, very dark...here's the book blurb and some sample chapters...

Fakes, Freaks, Cheats, Liars and Celebrities

Fame. Lies. Scandal. Drugs. Sex. *MURDER*. Celebrities have secrets to die for.

Andrew Manning has spent 20 years saving celebrities from the consequences of their own bad behavior and is known in the business as' The King of Scandal'. But now some particularly difficult and demanding characters are about strain even his legendary abilities:

Shelley, model and fashion icon, who's determined not just to blackmail her equally famous husband but also to destroy him.

Joey, an insecure reality TV star, desperate to hang on to his celebrity, even if it means slowly poisoning himself to death.

The Producer, a king in the world of entertainment and a serial abuser of hopeful young wannabe's. But this time he's picked the wrong girl for his perverted pleasures. Charlie, morbidly obese, murderous mafiosi adviser to... Janey, pop music goddess, a celebrity with peculiarly sharp teeth and disturbing eating habits that are about to be revealed to the public by an ambitious young paparazzo.

And then there's Johnny, Andrew's partner, a psychopath with a heart of gold who's on a mission to murder as many celebrities as possible.

Will Andrew be able to reconcile the demands of so many different and desperate characters, and who's going to end up dead?

And here's a sample chapter from 'Fakes, Freaks, Cheats, Liars and Celebrities' in which we meet foul-mouthed, homophobic Shelley. Shelley, model, singer and social media influencer, wants Andrew to blackmail her famous, secretly gay football star husband into giving her a huge divorce settlement, but Shelley has her own dark secret...

SHELLEY. TIME FOR A QUICK SMOKE?

Finally, the slow and tedious drive through London's crawling traffic is over and Shelley arrives at Anthea's house in Holland Park, she always stays there when she's in London. She and Anthea are Best Friends Forever. They've known each other since way back, from when they were in "Girls Gone Wild." There were four girls in the (quite successful at the time) band but Shelley only ever really liked Anthea. Chardonnay and Alicia were bitches and cunts, and where they fuck are they now? Losers! They hadn't been smart, but Anthea and Shelley had been. Shelley had used the band as a base from which to start her solo career, Anthea had exploited her celebrity and good looks to grab herself an extremely ugly but ridiculously rich banker. Christ, Shelley can feel nothing but admiration for the way she played that prick! Led him by the fucking nose, married him, stuck with him for a couple of years, then divorced him, taking almost everything he had. Honestly, men can be such gullible dickheads, show them a bit of tit and a glimpse of snatch and, in no time at all, you can have them behaving like well-trained dogs!

Once inside Anthea's house (she has her own key, that's how BFF she and Anthea are), she makes straight for the beautiful living room and throws herself into a gorgeous sofa, dropping her Prada bag onto a gorgeous coffee table, which rests on a gorgeous carpet. Shelley *really* likes Anthea's place, she makes her mind up that she too will buy a home in Holland Park when the divorce money comes through from Jack faggotpants.

Yes, the divorce settlement, more money, more success…what a wonderful day it's been! It's going to be so great when Anthea gets back from her latest shopping trip. Shelley can't wait to tell her what's about to happen to Jack, how she's about to blackmail him into a *huge* pay out. Hah, she is *so* going to screw him! Nobody fucks with Shelley!

Shelley muses happily for some minutes about her upcoming freedom from Jack and her fabulous future career in America, until her thoughts stray, unstoppably, to that package, nestled comfortably in the Prada bag. She takes it out, rolls it around in her hands, a greedy and needing expression on her face. Using her sharp finger nails, she quickly tears at and then unwraps the cellophane from the package, to reveal a substantial, round rock of crack cocaine. She places the rock of crack on Anthea's gorgeous coffee table. Taking a nail file from her handbag she begins to chip away at the off-white coloured lump, which has a texture somewhere between wax and brittle plastic. Expertly she detaches smaller rocks from the main block, each new rock just the right size for a single good hit when smoked. There's loads of crack here, enough to last her and Anthea a couple of nights, if they don't go too mad! As well as BFFs, she and Anthea are also BDBs, Best Drug Buddies.

She loves her crack does Shelley, fantastic stuff. Okay, so maybe the next day you might feel a bit down, a bit paranoid, but nothing that can't be smoothed out with a few drinks. Or some more crack. And the hit, Christ the hit! Once felt never forgotten! She knows of course that she shouldn't really be smoking it, what with her being famous, rich and beautiful and in a responsible position due to her influence over the young people of the world, but the public just doesn't realise that being famous, rich and beautiful is very hard work. Every day is filled with questions. What should I wear? Am I slim enough? How's my make-up today? Have I got the right handbag for this or that occasion? Who should I be *seen* to be speaking to? Which party do I go to, and which should I snub? Where should I be this afternoon to stand the best chance of being papped? These are all difficult and complex questions. Being a celeb is a demanding business, not everybody can handle it. Her lifestyle involves a lot of a pressure, and the crack is Shelley's way of relaxing, of dealing with the stress she endures every day. She deserves it. She is *entitled* to it.

Of course she has been in trouble with the crack before, resulting in some fairly unpleasant media coverage, but she had dealt with that, although it did involve some help from that hideous queer, Andrew. But that's all in the past. She's much more careful now, more discreet, she'll never be caught again. "Never say never," says a little voice somewhere in the back of Shelley's head, but she chooses to ignore it.

Shelley wonders if she should smoke a quick rock before Anthea gets back? Why the hell not!

'Fakes, Freaks, Cheats, Liars and Celebrities' is available to buy now as an ebook and paperback.

Printed in Great Britain
by Amazon